John Ogden

Paint it Jack

First Edition published 2024 by
Wilfred Books

This is a work of fiction and any resemblance to any
person living or dead is purely coincidental. The place
names mentioned are real but have no connection with
the events in this book.

Printed in Great Britain by McRay Press

A CIP catalogue record for this book is available

from the British Library

ISBN 978-0-9927-4313-0

This book is dedicated to my parents Beattie and Jack, to my children Polly and Charlie and to my wife Janet.

You are the light.

Contents

Chapter One

It was early afternoon and I was in a city centre café, the type of place where shoppers waddle in with their plunder, and hope to be revived by coffee and cake, or for the truly adventurous something cooked. The summer had long faded and the customers' clothes had run from the bright, the tropical, the revealing and the garish to the all-enveloping autumn shadows of grey, brown, and black.

I was sitting on my own having raised a few quid for a hot drink and a brief respite from the streets. I was nursing my phantom leg and the ghosts in my head when a loud, humourless family of three sat down at the adjoining table. Their every syllable and every glance were a complaint: the place was too full, it had no atmosphere, the menu was too limited, their food was taking too long to come. Theirs was a constant grumble of discontent.

The youngest member of the party was a young woman in her early twenties, dark haired with brown eyes. The first plate to arrive was taken by who I presume was Dad. It was a dull-looking plate of poached eggs on toast, there were complaints – obviously – about how pale the toast was, the fact it had been cut into triangles, the size of the eggs and the fact they had been overdone, not something I would have thought possible but then, as an ex-soldier, my taste buds and expectations had been conditioned by years of Royal Catering Corp carnage.

It transpired that "daughter" had ordered the same. Now, I was raised by a man of a certain generation to whom the principle of women and children first applied - into lifeboats, through doors and when food is delivered. But this Dad would have been the very first person to leave the Titanic. He leapt into his lunch, cutlery flailing like a ninja. I was pierced by the look of disappointment in her brown eyes, the same colour as those of my estranged daughter.

I had no newspaper to hide behind. No smart phone to tap and swipe as a substitute for thinking or doing. All I had were my own thoughts and my own sadness. Imperfect me would have given the first plate to my daughter. Imperfect me would have cherished every second spent in her company, not boorishly chewed through, and ignored all attempts at conversation. Imperfect me cried. I tried to stop it but I could not, these tears had taken so long they were distilled into a broken spirit. The youngster at the adjoining table, with the facial range of a mime artist gurned, elbowed her parents, and raised her perfect drawn on eyebrows scornfully at this sad sack. A memory from an old book by Leo Buscaglia blew back into my mind "Too often we underestimate the power of a touch, a smile, a kind word, a listening ear, an honest compliment, or the smallest act of caring, all of which have the potential to turn a life around." The reverse is also true, a small act of spite can cause the greatest hurt.

In my befuddled mind I was being rejected not by some anonymous, slack-jawed and dead-eyed stranger but by my own daughter. The trio were now all gawping. My eyes flooded and

I gathered what little I had, abandoned my seat, and stumbled for the door.

Do all lost souls seek the sea? This one did. On my way towards the harbour mouth my unsteady steps had crossed the path of a low flying mobility scooter. The driver did not stop and sped off towards his next victim, leaving behind an unbecoming trail of curses. In the midst of the expletives was an accusation that I was drunk or off my head, I was not either. Yet.

I found a quiet space and sat alone in shadow, almost sinking into the cool, ancient stone of the blockhouse. My combat trousers and scuffed boots hid the lower half of my body while a green waterproof, encroaching hair, and the straggle of a beard covered my top half. I was rapidly becoming weed covered waste ground. There was nothing to see or be seen here. I planned for there to be even less soon, apart perhaps from a chalk outline. But then, I had already been a silhouette for a while.

There was a clink as the contents of an outer pocket nudged keys that would turn no more. I emptied the contents of another pocket onto the stone ledge where the dimpled bottle seemed to bring all of the world into focus. "To see all the world in a grain of sand, and to see all fall from my own hand" William Blake's words seemed apt as I now intended to leave this, perhaps the only, world. The acrid, cheap scent of a grandly named discount whisky bolted from the open bottle. I squeezed white pill after white pill from their blister packs. Opposable thumbs – one flesh, one not - working, combining, to help me to lose my grip. Each pill was accompanied by an onomatopoeic scr-pop, like a dry twig breaking on a leafy forest floor, before each was carefully placed into one of three tiny wall-like piles.

In the harbour a large white, light-speckled ship was creeping towards the open sea. It was an uncommonly hot and febrile October, so the decks were lined with holidaymakers waving randomly into the dark, perhaps hoping that somebody might wave back. I raised my bottle, knowing that this "whisky drinking night owl" – a half-remembered lyric - would never "soar with the eagles the next day". Random lyrics and lines from books were forever mangled in my mind.

Boxes emptied. How strange that what could so easily kill you was piled high, in the company of other killers, in every chemist and convenience store. It was then that I regretted buying the cheaper generic ones whose edges are rougher, sharper and catch in the throat. A large glug of rough whisky and eight pills. Then a splutter and a dry, hacking cough as my body tried to close the bridge between head and neck, feeling it deserved better, and resisting the assault.

Tears navigated their way down my cheeks, through the wrinkles, lines, and scars, over the briarwood of my beard before pooling together on the longest wisps, and holding watery hands before leaping.

The ship, which was the "The Pride of somewhere or other" – and what an underwhelming place it must be, to be proud of a floating, rusting diesel engine - drifted past on its way towards somewhere in Northern France. My schoolboy French, once reasonable, made a fleeting appearance. "Salut" I toasted the disappearing hulk, before I swallowed more succour.

There was then rain, a fine, unconvincing supply-teacher like rain, before a hint of petrichor, clinging on although summer had long since gone. Scent may be the last human sense to go before we die. Perhaps it was my larger than average nose which imbibed more than its fair share which now triggered memories of new rain on a warm nights, of music, youth and freedom.

As I swallowed more the world around me began to blur. My clouded eyes saw dark silhouettes emerge from the shadows. There were square shouldered brutes in suits who lumbered, their legs heavy, feet pummelling the pavement. Was it a dream or did ghouls really gather close by with their shrieks of pain and evil laughter? A group of the undead wide-eyed, gaping mouthed and blood stained, joined the others. Across the flat clear common they all swept, overseen by the stare of the unmellow yellow Hunter's moon with its edges bruised as though nipped by a jealous sibling. As always, the dogs recognised the danger, their senses honed by thousands of years of living with the strange creature called man. Some hounds, out for their twilight toilet, especially the smaller yappers, stood their ground at least for a while, against the forces of darkness. Most others dragged their blanched, bewildered owners sideways towards the nearest tree, billboard or boarded seaside shack seeking sanctuary in shadow.

The crowd funnelled towards a green and purple light. By the door stood a solid stump of a man dressed from head to toe in black, his bullet head shaven, swirling tattoos storming around each forearm, muscles bulging unnaturally. A small translucent snake coiled around one ear whispering, instructing. On his breast a symbol, an emblem encased in a transparent sheath, letters conjoining to form the word which strikes fear, and makes even the most bended back straighten respectfully. "Security" it said. The Stump glared at the crowd, taking in every tiny detail. He then beckoned with a miniscule movement of his bullet-head towards the door, reluctantly agreeing that they enter. Above, creaking in the onshore breeze was an idealised painting of a jolly pub, and trollied customers – The Welcome Inn. On the windows were gaudy signs advertising cut-price drinks and offering prizes for the best fancy-dress costume.

It was then I realised I was in the middle of Halloween, a night just like any other, a mixture of frivolity, fate, and fear.

I could not now remember the band, or even the tune of the particular song, but the fragment of the lyric had caught like sheep wool on a fence "Give me a kiss with your apocalypse." My mind wandered to an image of the four horsemen each sporting crimsoned Marilyn lips. Pestilence seemed well suited whereas pale-horsed Death huffed, perhaps aware that glamour undermined the seriousness of his noble calling. The image faded.

Beneath me, the sea began to swell, the ripples becoming a roar. Tonight, there would be many a rough crossing.

Light on water has always fascinated me. The sea and the sky are forever changing, and when they are lit with beacons, ship lights and stars they are a scene in which I can lose myself. It may have been just a second, probably a few minutes, no longer as I don't recall a chime which would have woken me. However long, my contemplation was broken by someone ambling in my direction. When you survive on the street you dread the deliberate approach. There is always an offer involved: of an opinion, of violence, of mercy, money, food, or redemption. I wanted none of them. I hunched and stared towards the Isle of Wight, a useful way of avoiding excitement.

The ambler did not take the hint.

I steeled myself for whatever tirade this stranger cared to direct towards me. I had heard most of what normal people thought of folk like me, of what we should do, their criticism of our life choices and where we should go. "Not now, not ever" my inner voice became audible, and repetitive. The stranger, a somewhat shaggy man in a brown coat, came closer. *"Excuse me"* he said with no apology meant. He eyed the dimpled bottle which I pulled close; I had neither the time nor the drink to share.

"No thank you" my sentence starting and finishing before our eyes made contact. *"But I haven't even…"* he responded. "You will though" my whip smart response.

Our eyes then made contact, a mistake, I could now no longer ignore him.

"I'm alright, can you please just go away?"

Although I turned back towards the Solent, with dragging footsteps he advanced. I looked again. Now streetlight lit, I saw more than the coat for the first time. He had an intense face with penetrating eyes and a head topped with thick dark hair, tied behind. Not the usual type to lecture me. He held up his hands to indicate that I should not fear him. *"There have been others"* he said in a soft sing-song accent, Irish? Welsh? *"They all tried to make me go away, but some weren't as polite as yourself."*

He took two steps forward.

I bristled, my voice thickening, indignant. "Sorry fella, could you please just leave me alone?" I went to stand to reinforce the point, but my one pins-and-needle numbed leg buckled beneath me. From the ground.

"I don't want to talk to anyone right now."

The brown coated stranger edged forward and motioned towards the pile of pills.

"Aye, I can see that you've been to the physician, and it would appear that you have a mighty malady." A pause. *"From the look of things, you don't want to talk to anyone now, or forever."*

Brown Coat sat by the wall.

"It's none of your business." I rose unsteadily, booze and pills muddling my mind, my right hand clenched as I lurched forward.

The shaggy, boyish faced man smiled, wide and wider, his lips and teeth forming a gleaming, glimmering grin.

"I don't think you'll do me any harm young man, you're a few years too late for that."

"Why don't you just f…." It was then I fell face forward, my legs loose like a string-cut puppet. A boot caught, my ankle bent, and my outstretched arm scrabbled towards and then scuffed the wall, scattering the pile of pills, like so many white seeds, into the ever-hungry sea.

"Oh, that's a real shame" said Brown Coat insincerely *"At least you have still got some of that whisky. Do you mind if I?"*

I was now on all fours glaring though a haze of indignant intoxication at the shaggy man. "Look what you've done." I pleaded, gesturing at the now empty stone; its sacrifice swallowed.

"And what exactly have I done sir? Saved your life? Saved you from an eternity in Hell? Because if that is the case, you are being, if you do not mind me saying, less than grateful."

A cacophony of clocks then began to chime. Of the fifteen belltowers within earshot only four appeared to share the same time, the rest stumbled towards midnight like a glockenspiel rolling down a cobbled hill.

"St. George's will be next" there was a pause before a great wave of sound, a thunder of metal thrashing, crashing, and clanging which filled the harbour, and for one moment seemed to stun the city into silence.

The musical intermission was over.

"Grateful that you have interfered? Whatever I was or am doing has nothing to do with you." I again turned back towards the sea. He did not move away, but moved along the wall towards me. I wanted, I needed him to go, but he was not so easily dismissed. I succumbed to the last resort of the uncomfortable Englishman. Conversation.

"Thank you." I whispered, hoping that would draw our meeting to a close. But he was unmoved by gratitude, and unmoved.

"What do you, erm, do?" I asked, my usual sparkling wit and repartee having deserted me.

"Are you some sort of social worker or…?" I asked, spontaneously moving my now bloodied hands in the cupping, questioning way you do when words fail you.

Brown Coat smiled again. *"Well, I guess I try to do some good."*

Another pause.

"Do you work at the Dockyard?" The place was full with out of work actors attempting to bring history to life.

"Well, I did once upon a time, and I suppose I still do if you could call it that." He paused, as another distant clock marked time. *"Every night at midnight I remind those who care to listen that I have been and am still here."* There was a tone of permanence in the final word.

"Did you?" I gestured towards the bottle, the now empty blister packs, and the briny sea below that was busy ingesting more than the recommended dose.

"Once try to take my own life?"

He bristled, appearing resentful of the accusation.

"No, but in a way, I lost it, reclaimed it and now give it."

Well that explained everything!

In my head I said "Oh no, you are not one of those religious nutters that saves sozzled souls are you? Because if you are you can take your faith and stick it. It is people like you that knock on folk's doors first thing in the morning, pushing your leaflets and wanting to debate the meaning of life on a Sunday. For Christ's sake. When you hear the kettle boiling, or the radio don't you get the message we are not in?" I really wanted to swear, curse and scream because quite a few of my well-deserved lie-ins, albeit in a past life, had been disturbed by God botherers or delivery drivers with things I hadn't ordered. But the booze and the pills were sapping all of my energy.

All I could summon up to actually say out loud was a semi-polite "Well sod off, I'm not buying whatever you're selling."

I then sat on the wall watching the ferries, container ships and grey-hulled battleships as they drifted in the darkness. I was ruminating on whether all of those on board would make it to their destination, or would some give themselves up, and dive into the deep? On this autumn night, out in the Channel the sea would be ten degrees or so, so those who did not drown would soon succumb to the siren call of hypothermia. The shivering, the feeling of drunkenness, the joyful contradictory warmth as your body temperature lowers. At this moment, to me, death – whatever form it took - was far more welcome than life. And yet, here I was faced with a do-gooder who could not tell I was a lost cause and accept a "Not today thank you" before leaving to go knock on another door?

Brown Coat was still looking at me, now with more pity. He moved towards me shuffling along the wall. He kicked his legs like a bored schoolboy but his heels did not bounce off the stone. As I say this, I know you will draw your own conclusions, roll your eyes, and do whatever else you do when you don't quite know what you're seeing, such as, erm England winning a penalty shoot-out. Okay, so maybe football isn't your thing.

I had been drinking, but I swear that Brown Coat's legs moved through the wall as if it wasn't there.

You have probably seen mirages, or tricks of the light before. Even an English summer will cause pools of water to appear to float in mid-air. Well I have seen thousands of mirages - if you look closely you can tell it isn't quite a solid object, because the edges always blur. But this was no trick of the light, the legs of my brown coated acquaintance had passed through the wall. I looked behind and around for the trickery of the one-eyed light of the movie projector, but in vain. And then a gull, a large raucous herring gull flew straight through him. Its' sharp, taunting call immediately silenced, its' dark wings paled, the bird then flew high and higher as though pursued.

He looked from the gull to me.

"What was it you saw?"

"It's Halloween" I mumbled "strange shit always happens."

What was next? Sawing a woman in half? Card tricks?

I put on my politest, yet most insistent voice and made one more attempt to get rid of him. "I appreciate you are, in your own way trying to help but, could you please leave me alone. I am too tired to talk." I also thought but didn't say "I also have my own mad man to contend with."

There was no movement, just more words. *"No, not yet, I have a tale for you."*

"Sorry Sir" I still hoped that my emphasised politeness would help deal with his insistence, "it's too late for once upon a time, and I am far too old for bedtime stories."

His entire face smiled. *"You think so, too late for stories. Even for you Will?"*

Every single hair on my body rose.

"How do you know…?"

"My friend, when you are dead you know everything." his words curled like smoke.

So, not a religious zealot, not a right-winger cursing me for cluttering the streets, not someone seeking physical activity – at least not yet anyway, not a do-gooder. Just a plain old-fashioned nutter who knows a few magic tricks, the names of the local churches, thinks he is a Halloween ghost and for some inexplicable reason knows my name. Why me?

The drugs and drink were catching, tripping, and holding me. My eyes were staring unable to blink, eyelids held apart by invisible matchsticks, my body fire then ice, sharp, prickly and red-hot at first before gradually enfolding calming, welcoming the all-encompassing cold.

Nervously, I stood, then fell, it was a slow-motion replay of a fall, a drunkard's forward roll but for me there was no "Ta, Da!" to accompany my gymnastic display, as I bounced forward onto the competition mat and awaited the scores of the judges. My heavy, hulking roll would be pointless.

What do I do? Run? That could be a problem right now. Shout for help? Who knows how that would end up, it could be worse. Or do I sit and listen attentively and politely before parting on good terms? The options were limited.

Brown coat sensed my change of tack; outwardly, at least – having now recovered from my fall - I was still, almost calm, expectant.

"So why are you here, and why did you stop me?"

"I have been here for many years. I have seen those who feel death is their only answer. Some I am able to save, but only those who have a glimmer of hope. Others, whose light is already extinguished, I help to close their eyes" a pause *"and I have closed so many eyes."* His voice now a whisper. *"I have seen so much death. But I have also seen love, faith, and courage. I have seen so much to know that to die cannot be the end of everything."*

"And how can you be so certain about that?" A good argument always invigorated me, especially when under the influence…

"I knew there was something you were hiding beneath that camouflage. You have a mind. That is a beginning."

"Don't patronise me!"

"Sorry if I caused offence. I do tend to speak the truth, in fact, I pride myself on being quite honest." Another smile, I still was not re-assured and hoped to escape.

"I don't want to waste anymore of your time."

"Sir, I have all the time in the world," he gestured, encompassing all around and above, *"and your face, perhaps the most honest face I have ever seen seems most troubled. And if my eyes do not deceive, you seem to wish for time, as it ticks on this temporal plane, to disappear. Why is that so?"*

I responded with a shrug, and a mumble "I don't intend to sit here and bare my soul to a complete stranger."

"Well, perhaps we should become acquainted." He remained.

I sighed, "Well, if you want to talk, why don't you go first. Tell me about yourself. Who are you?"

"Willingly, I am, erm was, known by many names, perhaps the most famous of which is" he spoke slowly and deliberately *"Jack the Painter."* He paused waiting for recognition and a torrent of questions. No, there was nothing from me. He continued nonplussed. *"Although my trade gave me the name by which the public knew me, it is perhaps the dullest part of my story."*

I rolled my raw, red eyes, and made that noise you do when bored, a nasal, almost melodic hum, with closed mouth and clenched teeth – a num?

"I too know Portsmouth." began Jack.

This was not going to be gripping.

I num-ed twice more.

Sensing his audience wasn't in his thrall, Jack changed tack.

"Unlike you friend, I made a success of dying."

I glared at the few remaining pills and with my eyes traced the path their colleagues had taken over the edge. Did I point out the irony that he had been allowed to die? I concluded that I couldn't really be bothered.

"Well, that's as maybe. But we all get there in the end."

Jack stretched out his hand to accept a point well made, and continued.

"Some deaths are however a little more noticeable. Mine was the stuff of legend."

These days people use the word legendary in such an everyday fashion to describe mundane burgers, footballers of limited ability and even Kevin down the pub who can still stand after ten pints. In my experience anyone who calls themselves a legend, isn't.

I wasn't in the mood, although usually polite, there are times when you get to the end of your tether…

"Fuck off fella! Find someone else to share your delusions with. I have had enough of…" My words trailed off, and I once again turned towards the sea.

He continued, regardless of my outburst.

"It was just over there" he pointed. *"Many, many years ago. I used to count, but time passes whether you put a number to it or not. Just behind those lights, on The Hard."* His voice slowed as if he was struggling with a memory, for the first time he looked pensive.

"It was HMS Aresthusa, which had the tallest mizzen mast in the Royal Navy. She was a truly beautiful ship, captured from the French. Strange name though, that of a nymph who in order to avoid an amorous god is turned to mist, not your usual heroic bluster. There was, of course" his voice had regained its rhythm *"a great crowd, shouting, jeering, singing, they were a ghoulish lot. As was the custom, the hangman had auctioned my shirt, my then infamous brown coat, and my shoes. He made eighty guineas that day. There are always those who profit from the misery of others and an abundance of superstitious souls who ignore the irony and believe a hanged man's clothing and body parts will bring them luck."* A smile, *"Nobody wanted my breeches mind you. I suppose you understand why?"*

My eyebrows must have risen quizzically.

"Well, it's because when your neck breaks, you lose control of all the muscles in your body, and…"

"Enough!"

"It was the 10ᵗʰ of March, a bright spring day, and I remember it like it was yesterday, which in a way it was. At half past one, I was hoisted aloft by scores of men, the rope bit bull terrier like, locking tight, but there was no quick death. I hung in agony for many long

minutes before the end."

On the streets I had discovered that everyone has a story, they need it to get from day to day; the fact there was a tale did not surprise me, the intensity of the telling did.

"But you seem very much alive to me Sir. After all, we are talking and if you were a ghost wouldn't you be limited to clinking chains, blood-curdling screams, moaning, shrieks, and spectral groans?"

His eyes smiled. *"You've never met a real ghost before, have you?"*

"Erm, no." Such was my frame of mind if I could have, I would have run, probably screaming. As it was, I merely tried to sit up and unwind my cramped, pins and needled leg and its companion. I was trying to concentrate but every thought was caught on the barbed wire of drink, pills, disbelief, annoyance, and a growing fragment of fear.

"Spirits can only occupy the paths they made while living; although we are of air, we are earth bound. Immortal yet imprisoned. It is why some of the more restless ones draw attention to themselves, they throw, curse, and howl. They are not necessarily evil, indeed many of my fellows are merely bored. That said, some of the unsettled souls are truly demonic only avoiding – perhaps temporarily – an eternity of pain because of small-print and the actions of their codicillian counsel, or who they know." I must have shaken my head. *"You seem surprised, but even in death backs, albeit bony, are scratched."*

By his, I was going to say body language, let me say demeanour, my new friend was settled in for a lengthy discourse. He was not going to go away, was he? Whatever plans I had for the rest of the evening, death, and nothingness, would have to be put on hold.

"So, friend, why do you wish to talk to me. I am a" I paused "nobody."

"Will you delude yourself you always have."

"My mind is…"

He interrupted *"…A volcano, and you were, when I chanced along, throwing yourself into its cupola, surrendering."*

"You have no idea what I feel."

"Aye, perhaps not, but there is much you cannot hide."

It had been a while since someone wanted to talk to, and not at, me.

"But by your own admission you were hanged here. You must have committed a crime. After all, why else?"

"Ah, if you would like I will share my story."

Well, what else could I do but agree?

Chapter Two

Perhaps a little surprisingly there was not an immediate torrent of words, and embellished events. It was as though he was waiting for me to begin, for my own questions to uncork his bottle.

I started, as I so often do with the most obvious question, bluntly asked. "So, they hanged you, why?"

"Indeed, I was executed at the scene of my most famous action, not crime you note, although that was the contention of the judge, the Prime Minister and even the King – all of them disagreed with me on that. I was a soldier who died as a villain. Dangling sixty-four feet high above a crowd of twenty thousand."

There was a sardonic twitch of his lips, and I thought I saw him rub his neck, but the night was dark.

"But I was no villain sir. My actions were those of a God-fearing man. I had seen and wished to bring an end to horror. "On this mountain the Lord of hosts…will destroy…the shroud that is cast over all peoples, the sheet that is spread over all nations." From this place" He gestured towards the harbour. *"that shroud sailed in wooden ships."*

"Sorry," Jack looked at my bemused face, *"at school we were taught by a cane to memorise verses such as that one from Isaiah. I had little use for them at the time, but as one gets older you appreciate their value."* he smiled, eyes crinkling.

"The aforementioned verse tells of choirs of singing angels wishing peace on earth, goodwill to all men, and the end of death. In my short life, I never saw much peace, only, rarely, a promise of it. So, I tried in my own way to be a pacifier, and I paid the price. I am not sure that I was ever blessed, but, if I had my life again, I would do exactly the same but better, perhaps I would once again fail, but I would fail better." He gazed at me checking for signs of boredom, disinterest, or antagonism, but I was too tired and befuddled for anything which required effort.

"My purpose was to strive to make wars cease, to break the bow, shatter the spear and burn the shields with fire. I used my every effort to make the warmongers quake, to be still and know the power of God. I died fighting, but dying for peace is the most worthy death."

It may have been a trick of the sickly spectrum of neon and the glare of streetlight but I was certain I saw veins throb in Jack's neck and sweat form on his ghostly brow.

"I had seen soldiers torch houses, and then shoot or bayonet old men, women and children who tried to escape. I had seen scarlet coats soaked with the blood of scores of innocents. Then I was in the shadows, frozen and impotent with fear while screams scorched the air.

Sound stays longest in the memory, that of blade through flesh is one I pray I could banish from my mind. Scent lingers too, that of charred flesh and hopelessness as all you have and love are consumed by flame." Words tumbled from him ever faster.

"I witnessed an incredible slaughter, as those damned Hessians brought Hell where once was Eden."

Unless you are a doctor, nurse, priest, or homeless you probably see very little truth in life. People talk, type and text but rarely say what they truly mean. That night a spirit shared his soul with me, he was seeking redemption.

But there are times in life, those ticks of the clock when the thing to do is talk. But as a man, although you know what is right you ignore, evade, mock, and ridicule any suggestion of it; you are the product of decades of indoctrination.

"I can't" words stumbled from me "I have enough problems of my own. I am the wrong person to help with yours." I braced myself against the rough wall, looking to rise, to leave. "I am sorry." Ah, the default phrase of any Englishman in a difficult position.

"Do you not believe that I am dead? Do you not believe my tale?" Jack sounded pissed off, as if although immortal he had wasted his precious time talking to me.

I was given an appraising look which was less than complimentary.

"Being dead" he continued, blocking my teetering steps, *"I now know <u>everything</u>: that is the true burden of the undead, not remorseless immortality. We know many things we would rather not. This place, this patch of earth which binds me is full of troubles. Boys sail away, some come back, changed on the outside taller, brawnier, tattooed – for which I have never understood the*

attraction – but it is in the head where change is heaviest."

His gaze – no that is too weak a word – his stare, no, his eyes themselves seemed to bore through me.

"You are not alone, everyone's spirit is divided, some chasms are deeper than others."

More platitudes and generalisations, was he after all just some religious zealot wanting to catch me in his net? I once again reached for the wall, which seemed cooler and clearer than before. I pushed up but my muscles struggled to defy drug's and drink's gravity. A shake of his head.

"For instance, I know that on one mission you ran away, that you deserted your post; you had your duty, but you could not pull the trigger. You lied about what you could and could not see.

Two weeks later, that man, whose young daughter was at his feet when you had him in your sights made a bomb. But he, unlike you, had no compassion, and his explosion killed a bus full of schoolchildren, scores of innocents.

I know that haunts you. You hold on to the image of the mangle of steel, the tarnished stripped metal, with every scrap of everything that could burn gone. The bus bomb-bent and crumpled, twisted as though it had thrown up its own hands to hide from the horror, folded in from every angle. No sign of the children, apart from one solitary school bag, bedecked with rainbows and unicorns, which had somehow been flung from the wreckage."

No one knew, no one could have known. There were Taliban in the area, others attested to that, the target was too well protected, if I had gone ahead, I would have given away my position, and Phil and I would no doubt have been killed, or worse. They were the words in my report. Weeks before, the Americans aboard their helicopter gunships had killed 17 civilians, many of which were related in the tangled web of families to the Afghan President. We had to exercise care, everyone knew that…

No one knew about the young girl in the white dress. No one knew that she looked straight at me, closing the seven hundred metres between us in a glance which stilled my tremulous trigger finger.

No one knew that those eyes with their silent cry for compassion caused me to terminate my mission.

No one could have known.

No one even ventured to guess.

No one apart from the mad man in my head knew the truth.

Had this man taken form? Was he now before my eyes cloaked in brown?

"STOP!

    STOP!

        STOP!

            STOP!

Demon, go, leave me alone!"

Jack stayed, stock-still. His eyes unflinching, but now with a sympathy I had not noticed before. I could bend and crumple, I could flee or I could talk. I chose the latter. Something I had not done for so long.

Chapter Three

My words began "I have always been prone to melancholy. Not every day, and not always, in fact I can go weeks and months without being bitten by the black dog, although I sense it always walking right beside me. But, throughout my whole life there have been times when each and every light inside and outside of me has gone out. Times when there is no spark, no glow, no flame, merely dead embers, raked over coals with no heat or light or life to give. It feels as if I am trapped in a mine whose roof and floor are squeezing me, crushing together in a vice like grip. Times when whatever dim, distant guiding light had ever shone is forever gone.

On these days my head is part mush, part cotton wool, part firework. I see only shadows, which collude and plot with me as their intended victim. On these days, there is anger, and anger is all. It swamps, drowns, and suffocates me. I cannot breathe deeply to relax my troubled soul. I can only exhale, but with each gasp a small part of me dies.

I want, I hope, I pray for a time, *the* time, when tears are gone and the pain I feel is finally over. What makes it worse is that I have also known the most wonderful days, which strike like a shaft of sun through cloud on an empty beach. They are fleeting, and they flee, but they exist; they are, no, perhaps they were within my grasp.

Who knows why my mood has always burned, why sun is so

readily replaced by thunder? There was nothing in my youth, no trauma, no family separation, no institutional violence; no, there was nothing in my youth.

Where I come from you do not talk about your feelings; conversation tends to be limited to work, football, music, very occasionally politics and most often women. Men like me so rarely talk about our true feelings. We barely scratch that surface.

I cannot tell anyone what is happening right here inside this battered head of mine. It is not only that I am afraid to talk about my feelings, I just don't really know what they are. No one knows the real me, yours truly least of all. What people see is this grizzled exterior, a nut-hard face with commas for eyes, and a full stop for a mouth.

The conversation I had at the age of sixteen with the Careers Officer was short and to the point. Perhaps in some parts of the country or the world there are people in that job who have an extensive range of opportunities to share with eager teenagers who are keen to reach for the stars and do great things. Not in the North East, then or unfortunately now. For someone of my limited talents the CO suggested, in the five minutes generously allotted for the discussion on which my entire life would depend, that I could apply to the bank, the council or to the factory.

The latter was a monolith which squatted in a swirl of smoke on the outskirts of town. They made cookers, fridges, freezers, light fittings, and a myriad of other things. It was located close to home, and more importantly it was the place where I did not need to wear a tie. After five long school-uniformed years I resolved never – apart from weddings, funerals, and court appearances (although I was not planning a life of crime) - to wear a tie again.

The factory it was. I worked in the stores, the treasure trove where all of the bought in components were kept. There were ranks of racks, a plethora of baskets and small plastic bins. At first, I was given responsibility for screws, bolts, nuts, and washers. They were something I had not really thought about before. My Dad like most men his age had a large ex-coffee jar in which he kept everything that could be turned with a screwdriver, tightened with pliers, or hit with a hammer. Whenever a need arose to fix something, there was always an item in the jar that would do the job, although admittedly many things at home were either slightly askew or just nailed to the wall.

I soon learned that when it comes to assembling a refrigerator or a cooker there is limited room for manoeuvre, and not too many opportunities to use six-inch nails. I soon settled in, and a few years later was promoted. Even though I could not drive a car I was, after quite a few lessons and a nail biting (for the examiner) practical test, given a job with my own propane powered fork truck. Although it may have been bright yellow with a scarlet fuel tank, to me it was my mustang on which I rode the pot-holed prairie, emptying lorries of their loads of steel, carboys filled with some of the most toxic chemicals, fibreglass (which still causes me to itch just thinking about the stuff) and whatever else they delivered.

When needed, I was summoned by a radio which unfortunately only worked intermittently, usually failing to function when I was deep in conversation with someone particularly interesting, or female, or more often both. When the summoner failed to contact me on the radio an announcement would be made via the booming Tannoy system, interrupting the stream of pop music which was played to keep us employees happy. Mornings were punctuated by the "Our Tune" feature with its mournful theme music. A listener would write in telling their tale of woe, the feature always ended with the playing of a piece of heart-rending reflective music which was usually in a minor key and accompanied by all round gentle sobbing. You could hear a pin drop at 10:15 every morning.

My job was the envy of everyone who was tied to a production line. Unlike them, to an extent I had the freedom to choose what I wanted to do and when to do it. I was a free spirit riding the range, a rebel without a cause in my own eyes, "a rebel without a clue" in the eyes of many others.

Unlike the other storemen in their dangly sleeved, slightly too short-legged burgundy dust coats (a source of much hilarity to the shop floor lot who would refer to the lads in the stores as plums, a euphemism for balls, and indeed they did usually go around in twos...) I wore a navy-blue set of overalls which, because of Mam's good efforts, had sleeves which did not fall into the canteen soup and legs which ended at the ankle. In a place of conformity, I stood out.

Now this had its good and bad points. Freedom to choose what

I did when and who I had interesting conversations with were the plusses. On the other hand weighing heavily was my boss, the man who ran stores and stock control, Alan Cook. His management style was decibel based. Some of us reckoned this was a form of echo location as he was – as evidenced by his bottle-bottomed glasses – more than a bit short sighted.

Mr. Cook (never Alan to his face!) rather unfairly always wanted to know exactly where I was and what I was doing. Two pieces of information I was reluctant to share - not that I was particularly lazy, I just did not want to be managed.

I was constantly good enough, and at times great, at what I did, but I was always a bit aloof, as social as I needed to be but no more. I never joined in with Tuesday night football, or Friday afternoons (we finished at noon) in the pub. My colleagues were acquaintances at best, they were never friends, and when I look back on it now it was probably a deliberate act on my part. I decided early on that it was far better to be a constant outsider and avoid being mixed up in the troubles and heartbreaks of others. The factory worked for me for a while, but outside clouds began to gather: we were in the middle of another Tory recession, the company was facing more and more competition, its profits were squeezed, and there was a need for it rationalise. The latter a word which always seems misspelled to me, as it is always done in haste, more rash than rationale. Whatever, it was time to move on. That worked for me. I have nearly always wanted to be somewhere else.

Mr. Cook later joked that the day I picked up my redundancy cheque was the only time he knew where I really was.

Up until that point I had been able to avoid the family tradition which was went back six generations. As the eldest son, I – unless I had a proper job - at the age of twenty-five, was expected to join the Army. The Navy or Air Force were not options; in my now dead Grandad's opinion "well boats sink, and planes crash" and you cannot really argue with well researched logic like that. Having now left the factory, I had nothing to excuse me.

Jack nodded *"I sensed you had a restless spirit"* he said, *"please tell me more."*

"I was sure that I would fail whatever tests the Army placed in front of me; surely there must be something lying dormant within me that would get me off the hook and enable me to retreat honourably with a "Sorry Dad I tried…."

Although I did not want to die a young man's death; I just wanted to have something troublesome lurking in my guts that would cause the examining medic to purse their lips, click their tongue, give me the pitying look which is so well developed in the profession it must take a year or so of training, and then put a red cross where a green tick should be.

I tried. I slouched, coughed, and breathed heavily through my medical. I had even – after I had heard this approach had worked as a way of avoiding conscription in South Korea - stuffed myself silly with doughnuts, pizza, and ice cream for a good fortnight beforehand. Although this may have been unnecessary as there is a density, a certain heft to our family perhaps to stop us blowing away or being taken by eagles. Between us, my family had surprised many a set of scales, or in the case of my two sisters, their grooms who were keen – at least initially - to carry them over the threshold.

But the damned x-ray-eyed medic saw through my facade, giving me the impression that perhaps some other less than sincere volunteers had tried my ruse before. "A clean bill of health" he said "although" hinting at my own upholstery, "there's very little pizza and few doughnuts where you're going."

Basic training was a shock with its order, control, and systems. Some of us struggled: me with even more people telling me what to do, others with the distance from home. Over time strangers lost their strangeness. There were many of us young men with the same story, of not quite fitting in. Some came from fractured families with jumbles of surnames, others were like boats who were storm tossed with nothing to anchor them. Strangely, or perhaps not, there was one reference point, one place on the identity map where we either felt we belonged, or where others told us we should reside. The grid reference was accent. You put the British together, and within a smattering of sentences everyone is placed, referenced, and filed. We are defined, imprisoned, or liberated by how we speak.

They called me "Geordie." I am, or at least I used to be reasonably laid back about many things, but there are a few trigger points which cause me to rankle and respond. As you may already know Jack, there are many accents in the North-East each with their own music and notation. I've nothing against the good folks of Newcastle who are real Geordies, but I am from Durham so I am a Durhamite. I told my fellow squaddies of their error, and then immediately realised my own.

Whatever the academics say, there are no sharper minds, apart perhaps from a football crowd, than an army platoon. Almost instantly they wove my love of a French comic book dog – I had a 't' shirt with his picture - together with my categorical statements on language. Henceforth, my nickname was "Dogmatic," shortened, where needs be to a "Woof." It is amazing how upset soon turns to laughter, and separation to togetherness. Before the week was out, this jumble of random jigsaw pieces had formed a new picture, although one which would undergo a great deal of change before it was coherent and more straight edged. We might have been a bundle of broken and bruised souls, but we had the makings of a brotherhood.

I could then no longer be a distant observer; encouraged verbally, physically, and mentally my hard shell cracked as I gradually became something I had long resisted being - a member of a team. Of course, I had worked with others in the various jobs I had but there is a profound difference between task and duty. I had never even been particularly loyal to my favourite bands, I never bought every album, and as far as religion, well back then I had no allegiance in that department. So, this combination of duty and loyalty was new to me, born out of necessity perhaps, but there was something more.

Many of my comrades were in the army because of their disfunctional families, whatever that word means, after all, aren't all families - Royal, Royle or regular - screwed up in some way? Many of the lads were there because their world contained so little else. Since the more bittersweet of the two Elvis-es had sung of "the boys from the Mersey, and the Thames and the Tyne" most shipyards, pits, steelworks, and cotton mills had closed for good. We had become a country of proud "former" places – aye the media always use that prefix - where money was once made and flowed into the hands of the wealthy, but money and those who own it always move on. It and they are relentless.

Most of us were not exactly sure why we were in the Army. Some like me had a family tradition to uphold. Most just wanted to be somewhere other than where they came from for a while. And there were those who had swallowed the advertising slogan and wanted to "Be the best."

The thirty or so of us in my platoon soon became a sort of extended family. Some clever bloke once said there are two tests of friendship – whether you are prepared to lend someone a fiver, and whether you see a person more than twice a year – well I saw this lot far too often, and with maybe four exceptions, I would not lend these lads a penny. But they were *more* than friends, we would put our lives on the line for one another.

It was just another chapter for us all, and that is all it was until it became its own story."

40

Jack nodded.

"Will, my friend, thank you for telling me your tale, I sense there is much more to tell, could you please continue?."

Chapter Four

I did indeed carry on, it felt good to release my words into the cold night air.

"My Grandad regularly went hunting for rabbits and I sometimes accompanied him. Throughout my childhood I begged him to let me shoot his trusty air rifle. He told me I was too young, and that you need to be strong to shoot straight and true so the animals don't suffer. He died before I was strong enough. It was a few years after his passing, at the funfair of The Durham Big Meeting, better known as The Miners' Gala when I first shot a rifle. It was chained down like an unruly dog, and fired tiny lead pellets through a slightly twisted barrel beneath deliberately offset sights. But I had always been good with puzzles. After two ranging shots I figured out that it shot left and low. Within a minute I had compensated for the carney's challenge and made a fat hole in the centre of the paper target. A large pink bunny was my prize, which I swiftly gifted to my then girlfriend who carried it together with a wonderfully flushed expression of pride and embarrassment for the rest of the day.

On the army shooting range there were however no pink bunnies, or at least none were visible; just a ditch, sandbanks, a wall, and targets of concentric circles of red, black, and white, and further back an image of an on-rushing monochrome marauder. After the barked safety drill, we were each given a gun, a surprisingly heavy dense semi-automatic weapon with a bewildering array of etchings and things to adjust, a steel cigarette packet-like magazine and forty rounds. We were pointed in the right direction, we loaded and began.

The noise, like a succession of empty wardrobes falling down a short flight of concrete stairs, was deafening. We first shot at 100 metres, in a range of firing positions – prone, crouched, standing - then the same at 200 metres where we also shot, standing supported, firing whilst leaning against a post. Finally, the range was 300 metres where we fired in just the prone position. We all fired together, most of us at our respective targets.

The instructor's binoculars gazed bug-eyed at the targets, some of which had been frightened but still unmarked, some were grazed, others perforated, and mine, yes, mine was shredded. "Let's try 300 metres, again shall we?" was the non-negotiable question. More rounds, more squeezing, and more shredding. Forty plus another forty pieces of lead left me, and every single one found its target. Eyebrows were raised.

So, some months later there I am in a foreign land fighting for my own country. I am crouched down on a desolate hillside, thermal underwear beneath my dust encrusted uniform keeping out the searing night cold, and wicking away pools of day sweat. I am gazing down on a farmyard where chickens fluff, peck, scratch, and strut around. The resting engines of three trucks are pinging as they cool. A door jerks open and three men amble into the yard sending the chickens scurrying and squawking in a cloud of dust and disgruntlement. I squeeze six times, three lives end. The radio crackles, I report and retreat.

My role is executioner. A Pierrepoint with a long-range rifle, but unlike the infamous hangman there is no shaking of the condemned man's hand, just a signal from my spotter before Larry and I do our work. I am not usually one for giving inanimate objects names, although I know enough people who christen cars and in doing so bring an object into the family. I have never really seen the point. So why did I give my rifle a name? Well, a sniper is a mostly solitary, and invisible soul. This highly engineered composite of metal and plastic became my confidant, my accomplice and at times my conscience. The nickname was not wholly determined by the manufacturer describing what it did on its lethal tin, it harked back to a distant, much simpler, past.

The factory did not steal all of my dreams, and I was not always a *total* loner. About two years into my factory life I began to play the drums and then stumbled – via a random conversation with a stranger at a bus stop - into a band. There were four of us: two guitars, bass, and drums. We were called Larry & Company in homage to a legendary English thespian who had starred years before in a TV show in which the eldest member of the band was an extra. We played our songs of love and loss, of politics, fear, and hope for anyone who would listen. We were together for a year or two, a band of brothers (and indeed two were actual siblings: Peter and Paul), with me the taciturn, remote one. We eventually broke up as bands tend to do, there was a petty squabble over something or other, undoubtedly my fault as back then I used to be half-arsed about most things and argumentative about everything else. The others were far more ambitious and talented than I would ever be, they were those who dreamed in daylight.

Although we went our separate ways, we left a small, now almost impossible to find legacy, some songs which we recorded and issued to a great chorus of indifference. Our greatest achievement was perhaps the song "Thoughts from the backseat of my car" which legendary disk-jockey John Peel played a number of times on his national radio show. Some of the lyrics remain etched on my mind. "In dimming light unveiling, more things than I imagine, but don't rely on reason, there's more than that to live for." My drum kit clattered, thudded, splattered, splashed, and crashed in a speeding rumpus of different directions before driving the song to an emergency stop. Although I did not know it, perhaps I was at my happiest then, not relying on reason."

I paused awhile, reflecting on past happiness. My story continued.

"Each of Larry's shots was snare drum sharp with stick struck dead centre, with no drag, no ruff, no muffling to mute the note; even weapons of war make their own clear, precise, brutal music.

In some ways I had returned to that time with another ostensibly simple task, but one with its own rules and protocols. The band smaller now, a duo, just me with Phil, my spotter. A few years older, he was a rangy, goat-like bloke who had dreamed of becoming a weatherman when he was younger, but whose "A" level grades fell short of what he needed for university. He was most at home in the mountains, which were where he spent his leave, always returning with tales of peaks conquered. He very rarely talked about family, although there was the hint of a distant brother, and an argument that had never healed. In common with most mountaineers his dream was to climb Everest; he wanted to be so high that he could see the curve of the Earth, and light and darkness in one glance.

He was saving towards the fifty thousand pounds or so he needed. He would give me regular updates on how close he was. Sometimes he joked that he could of course, one day, just jack the army in, and casually saunter across the border into Pakistan, Kashmir and then Nepal. If only life was so simple.

He read too, travel books mostly. He wanted to see more of the world and explore the five directions of the Rig Veda – north, south, east, west, and here. When the world pushed in around us, he would talk of elsewhere, and when we felt windblown and bullet ridden, of the amazing sights that we had yet to see. "One day we will walk in the most beautiful places" was his refrain. "We will" became my semi-automatic, but no less heartfelt reply.

Phil would deal with the technicalities: range, relative humidity, barometric pressure, wind speed and details of the target which I would then double, sometimes treble check. Not because I didn't trust Phil, I did absolutely, but one mistake, one misjudgement would unravel our one and only chance.

Phil was my eyes and ears. When deployed both of us were covert and hidden in our curious lizard looking sand and rock coloured gillie suits, melding into the surrounding scrubland. Well, we might have been almost invisible to man but not to the extremes of heat and cold, and the tiny pinpricks and bites of those almost invisible parasites which targeted us as a source of moisture, warmth, and the rich, life-giving cocktail of blood.

We had worked together for a year or so when we received orders for our next mission. There was to be a wedding of a leading Taliban commander who Army Intelligence had been tracking for some time. Security would be tight around the venue – a farmhouse on the edge of Sangin town, just by the river. The sheer number of guests, many of whom were women and children, meant that the army could not launch a full-scale assault or even use a mechanical drone. What was needed was one of the few qualities which still separated us from machines, human precision. At base, Phil and I spent hours painstakingly reviewing maps and photographs to find the perfect spot from which to launch our attack.

The day before the wedding we arrived close to the site, then made our way to our destination. We dug in, camouflaged, hiding like hibernating animals, slowing our heart rates, and remaining perfectly still apart from our ever-seeing eyes. We were two hundred metres apart from one another, on a cliff above the river.

Since I was a teenager, I have always carried around books. I started out with fantasy novels, then classics, histories, some

– mostly comic – novels, and increasingly and much more recently, poetry books. I admire the poet's ability to fine tune so few words into something which helps us to know we are human and that every emotion we have has been experienced by others. To paraphrase Leonard Cohen, perhaps poetry is the "orange crate we hang onto in the flood."

As I prepare myself for war, as I order myself for chaos, as I place myself in my bubble, I quietly recite these few words from the Longfellow poem Hiawatha which tells the story of the Ojibwe hero.

"Take your bow, O Hiawatha,
Take your arrows, jasper-headed,
Take your war-club, Puggawaugun,
And your mittens, Minjekahwun,
And your birch-canoe for sailing,
And the oil of Mishe-Nahma,
So to smear its sides, that swiftly
You may pass the black pitch-water;
Slay this merciless magician,
Save the people from the fever
That he breathes across the fenlands."

We were there, we told ourselves, again and again until we almost believed it, to save the people of the world from the fever."

Chapter Five

"Aye, you have had a life, and you tell a good tale, but please before you go much further, could you please indulge me and let me share some of my own story."

My mind had tired with recalling and re-living the past; I welcomed the rest. Jack took a deep breath and sat by me.

"The first thing I remember is the smell; the foul, rank, rich smell of human excrement. It covered the streets, it splattered your clothes and your boots and if you were unlucky, or you were distracted, it fell on your head from the sky, from chamber pot clouds. There were many times I set out from home, only to arrive at my destination with my hair a different colour.

Edinburgh was a grim place; its nickname Old Reekie may have been related to the rank rain, or the showering shit I do not know for sure. My family, all fourteen of us, lived in Cowgate. Surrounded by slums so squalid, the very picture of hell, where only a very robust soul could grow up unharmed in the clenched fist of one of these blocks. We were near to the Grassmarket where every once in a while, usually on a saints' day, crowds would gather for a public hanging. There would be a holiday atmosphere with street stalls, musicians, jugglers, dancing bears, food, and drink. It was as if the whole world were conspiring to condemn the hanged men and remind them of the earthly joys they would no longer be able to experience.

It is a strange thing a hanging, it can take the speediest second or many minutes as though Death himself is undecided whether or not to take the miscreant.

So, my earliest memories are excrement and death. In many ways they were a signpost for my own life.

My father's blacksmith furnace was my favourite place, the intensity of the dry, metallic heat, the sweat on my father's brow and the clank and hiss as, like Vulcan, he brought life from dead rock. In the crowded city it was a place of safety where my siblings and I would gather to help in what little way we could – bringing water or fetching tools (some of them so heavy we could barely carry). We would watch the magic repeat time after time, and listen in to the tales which the traders, wheelwrights, soldiers, and travellers shared amongst the din of the anvil's chorus. At the age of seven my father died, the chorus stopped and our safe place vanished with him.

That year, I began school at George Heriot's Hospital. Of the one hundred and so boys there, many were the same as me; poor, fatherless but bright and lucky enough to be granted a scholarship by the charitable school which had been setup by Heriot, a rich goldsmith of the city for such unfortunates as ourselves. We were luckier than most as at least we were in school, and not at the mercy of the streets or some brutal employer. At first, our learning was basic; reading, writing, and arithmetic. Music, and Latin were soon added. We also learned how to pray. Five times a day, beseeching God to save us. He may well have saved some, but many died. It seemed as though not a month would go by without one of Heriot's boys passing on to the great beyond. Once a week, on Sunday at Greyfriar's Church

I would glimpse my family – my Mother increasingly aged beyond her years, and my eleven siblings. A glimpse was the only contact, the schoolmaster did not permit us to talk to our families, we had become pupils and were no longer sons."

Jack paused, as though straining to lift his memories. *"We were taught to be tractable and obedient to the advice and authority of our teachers, their instruction reinforced by buckle, belt, and cane. We were moulded to be solid citizens, to obey, to fit in, to know our place, and in accordance with the school motto "Impendo" to give cheerfully. We were trained to be little danger to either church or State. Perhaps what I have been fighting for my entire life and beyond is to show that I am indeed able and willing to disobey."*

"When I was young, I couldn't speak plainly," as if to emphasize this point, Jack carefully enunciated each word *"it was as though my thoughts were crowding and jostling before they stumbled over my tongue. I would stutter, pause, and then repeat what I had just attempted to say. Of course, my school mates understood and demonstrated all of the sympathy, kindness, and compassion you would expect of a pack of rabid, uniformed dogs. They called me "Ay, Ay, Ay, Ayyy" as though about to sneeze "Aitken." I never blessed them for that. That said, I was no angel when it came to pointing out the deficiencies of my fellow pupils. Minor deviations or deformities – jug ears, knock knees, acne, and many others – were exaggerated as though our childhood tongues were cartoonists' pens, although we were far more brutal.*

So, perhaps because of my own problems with speaking I admired those who could weave words and cast spells with syllables and sentences. Now I was never much enamoured with the church. The building was beautiful, it wrapped itself around you with its pale grey horizon and vivid, blue-painted sky. Sacred music at first a drone, and then with voices like massed birdsong would uplift you. But the beauty there was would be broken when someone began to speak.

The words spoken in that place were mostly pointless platitudes and tales of a jealous and judgmental God delivered in staccato Scots. What I thought did He, The Almighty, have to fear? Why did He demand praise? Was it perhaps a need which if not met would cause Him to cease to be? The prayer of humble access with its entreaties of "we are not worthy" reinforced feelings that if we were part of God's plan, our place in it was merely to praise and then to suffer. The wealthier members of the congregation were some of the city's worst villains yet on Sunday their holiness almost shone from their reserved pews.

So, what else do I remember from school, apart from the thin grey food, permanent cold, and the planting in me of a love of the stories told by the Roman poet Ovid? It is perhaps somewhat strange to tell that my strongest memories are the sermons I heard one particular Preacher utter on Sundays. This may surprise you as most homilies, I am sure you will agree, seem to be nothing beyond jumbles of words, exhortations, threats, and quotes from a book that everyone has, but few have read.

Reverend Erskine not only spoke well but seemed to have read parts of scripture which others either had not or had chosen to ignore or forget. Although there was always a whiff of brimstone and damnation in his words, there was also a breath of life. He told tales of a new world and a new beginning that was not mere apple-based myth. He had a knack for making life spring from a dry book, his recurring theme – when I think back, with the benefit of all I have learned since – was hope. He would share like an ancient wild-haired bard Old Testament stories of David, Esther, Joshua, Judith, and others with their victories against overwhelming odds, of despair sharpening invention, and finding a myriad of ways to fight against oppression. He spoke of the need for freedom and justice in this world now, he spoke of a promised land not after but before death and he sometimes spoke of the fine people of the Americas. It was only with hindsight that I realised how brave he was, after all it was only a few years since the Bonnie Prince Charlie and his Jacobite rising had been routed at Culloden. My boyish mind was transported from Edinburgh's cold gloom to the sunlit uplands of hope and opportunity. Prometheus-like, that preacher lit a fire in this boy's heart which was as bright as my father's furnace.

Against the background of a life of drudgery, Ovid's tales of change and rebirth and the sermons of Erskine entwined in my now teenage mind. I dreamed of one day becoming a hero."

There was something about Jack the storyteller which connected with me. It was his passion, and the sparkle still alive in his ghostly eye. He needed to tell his tale, and that night I needed to listen.

"You spoke of your own job a little while ago and the limited options you had. Well at the age of fifteen some of my fellow pupils – the

so-called "lads of parts" – those who had been able to demonstrate their potential - went off to university with the promise of one day becoming an officer in His Majesty's Army. This was a dream of mine; but I was not gifted, I did not have the parts, and my family were too poor to buy a commission. There was no adventure and excitement for me, instead, I was apprenticed as a house painter.

Oh yes it was a trade, but it was a poor one. My school masters said that they thought I would be suited to it as my maternal grandfather was himself a proud practitioner of this once specialist, skilled occupation. That may be true enough, but I know my masters also felt that I had a weak mind and limited capabilities. Whatever the reason, I was apprenticed to Master Painter John Bonner under whose tutelage I learned how to mix and prepare colours, to draw, and paint words and figures.

For the next five years I painted windows and doors very well indeed, but I excelled at sign painting. After a while it seemed that most of the shop fronts in Cowgate and beyond bore my handywork. Exhortations to buy beer, wine, and comestibles; my brush weaving its bristled magic and enticing people via images of foaming bottles, fresh green cabbages, and happy cows to visit shops and spend. After five colourful years in which I grew to know the city like the back of my hand, my master teaching me all he knew not only about the trade, but also about aspects of life which never featured in my schoolbooks. In hindsight, Master Bonner was my surrogate father, providing the guidance and discipline I needed. My pay contributed to the family's meagre coffers although my mother left me a little in my own pocket, it was enough to begin to enjoy the alehouses and other experiences of the city.

As I came towards the end of my apprenticeship Mr. Bonner's business began to struggle against the background of another economic slump. As a result my master had no alternative but to let me go. I left his employment with my roll of brushes and five pounds in my pocket. I considered staying in Edinburgh, but as there was no work I felt there was little point.

I was twenty years old with thirteen years of school and training behind me, I had a trade. It was time to move on.

So, I too left my hometown turning my thin, pale, etiolated - a description bestowed upon me by my French tutor - face towards the sun and headed south, along the Great North Road, towards the largest city in Europe, London. About ten times the size of Edinburgh it was a place of opportunity where fortunes could surely be made. For a while I naïvely believed the myth of it being a city where the streets were paved with gold. On my arrival I was very soon disabused of that notion.

It was not a place of peace in any sense of the word, after the relative quiet of the North Road the ever-present human noise was enervating. Houses of call were full of men seeking work but there was little to be had. My profession – they were all ranked by guilds and snobs from the genteel to the mean, nasty and stinking – was towards the bottom of the dung heap.

To defend myself, and what little I had, from the menacing and reckless scarabs which lurked on every dark street corner, I bought a cheap pair of pistols – as a Protestant, even if then a less than devout one, I could.

With little work, my own money soon went. The last straw a bill of mine unpaid by an apparently wealthy man who disputed the quality of my brushwork, we disagreed but he employed muscle whereas I had none. So, there was no call and no cash for my brush and paint. I did however soon find a use for my pistols.

Highwaymen have always had a reputation as dashing horsemen who steal from their unsuspecting victims and then gallop heroically into the gloom. And some no doubt were. As my father had shoed many I should have grown to love horses, but they always struck me as aloof, superior. Indeed one, a piebald ill-tempered creature had bitten me as a boy, I still have - no, had - the scar." Jack went to pull up his left sleeve, but it remained still. He smiled, as much to himself as to me before continuing. *"And of course, the wretched creatures tend to be rather recognisable and then there is the cost of stabling and such. So, this horse-avoiding painter became a highwayman who kept his feet firmly on the ground.*

It did not begin well. As I told you earlier, when I was at school, I struggled to speak clearly. Indeed, I stuttered terribly. Teachers thought me slow as I never answered quickly; even though my brain knew the answer and my arm would be raised before my classmates the words remained stuck in the great chasm between mind and tongue. Some masters thought me disrespectful and had me beaten. My fellow students, exploiting weakness mercilessly the way all children do, would taunt and tease. I would respond, I would fight, I would be reprimanded and beaten yet again. This casual violence combined with the institutionalised fagging where

I was forced to steal, and in-turn beat up fellow pupils, prepared me well for my later life. But even though I fitted in as best I could, we measure success by fluency, and because I stumbled over my words, I was seen by masters, pupils, and even to an extent by my friends as damaged, perhaps deranged, and thus deficient.

So, of course I put myself in a position where the ability to speak clearly is not just a prerequisite, but also a matter of life and death! There I am, on foot by a group of poplar trees on a road north from London, close to the Bull and Last tavern wrapped in the sanctuary of the heath, surrounded by the murmur of banks of tawny bracken. It is the night of my first highway robbery. In my mind, I had rehearsed this scene many times. The coach is approaching, the light in the casement by the driver casting shadows across the bracken and scrub. The brasses are jangling, and the hooves are pounding into the road. From the inside of the coach there is light, playful laughter.

Fifty yards away, I steel myself, thirty yards, twenty, I breathe deeply, raise my pistols, and open my mouth to bellow my instruction to "STAND AND DELIVER."

In reality, my bellow was not even a whisper, my mouth dried and my tongue tied.

The horses whizz past and I leap to the verge feeling their force and smelling their sweat. The burly coach driver sees me but as he thunders past he gives me a look of incomprehension mingled with pity. From inside the coach a young boy looked out at my open mouth and raised pistols; far from terrified, he smiles and waves!

But, once I had got the hang of it, being a highwayman came easy to me. It is a lot like painting in that it requires the necessary planning and preparation. But then again, to me everything is like painting. I would clear and smooth the site of the robbery: just the necessary number of obstacles to the oncoming coach, combined with the right mix of places to hide, clear sight lines and an escape route.

I bought a blunderbuss whose charge of rose petals and scented herbs I would fire into the air. The horses would immediately stop. The air would fill with the perfumed pyrotechnics before I called in a resounding - and somewhat easier to deliver – manner, my challenge of "HALT." Because of my deficiencies I had settled on a short, effective instruction. I would then train my pistols on the coach and its occupants.

Stories of the gallant, courteous, fragrant and (some said) flirtatious robber spread quickly. The authorities sought to catch me but as the only description they had was a vague picture of a red-haired, rather thin man with a Scottish accent, they did not know where to begin. There were thousands of us Scots in London living in the tangled web of its dirty streets. We were all subjected to hostility and prejudice, after all it was only thirty years or so since the Young Pretender had massed an army and marched south. Londoners despised us, and truth beknown we cared little for them. When the authorities, especially the loathed Bow Street Runners who were organised and encouraged by Sir John Fielding whose "duty obliged him to live in constant contention with the refuse of creation" came around asking questions they learned little from my Scottish kin, particularly as The Runners sought to capture and hang one of their own. Indeed, many, too many, of the bodies left hanging on the road-side gallows poles, whose hair was still discernible, and had not yet been blown or crow-pecked away, or even removed by the ghoulish or the superstitious, were red-headed Scottish men.

You could be hanged for anything in those days; perhaps this is a slight exaggeration, but there were over two hundred capital offences. If you stole bread to feed your family you would hang, if you caught a hare to feed your family you would hang, if you expressed your opinions by scrawling slogans on a wall you would also hang. As I said before, I had seen many men swing on the Edinburgh gallows, but London, ah London, was a different matter. Eight times a year they had mass executions up at Newgate. There were of course some who deserved to die, for murder or worse and they warranted their fate. But for many their main offence was having been born poor and for whom the stolen bread of life, became their bread of death.

Those eight days were like holidays and the roads to the gallows would throng with people jostling to see the prisoners as they approached in their open cart. Most folks would jeer and curse, some would throw rotting vegetables or worse, yet some would bow their heads and pray. All were thankful that it was not them, this time. The focus of the crowd was the gallows itself around which several thousand people would gather. The prisoners were executed in front of this riotous, noisy, scabrous congregation. The criminals' last moments were for all to see, the time when they made peace with whatever god they believed in, or the moments when they called or whispered their goodbyes to their loved ones, all was in plain sight. Diminished, mocked then killed. A ghastly morality play to entertain a ghoulish audience.

That said, there was one hanging which if I was ever unlucky enough to be caught, I wanted to emulate; that was the execution of one of my legendary predecessors Claude Duval. Ah, Duval! As you may know he was a gentleman highwayman who abhorred violence but loved music, dancing and flirtatious behaviour and so was loved by the ladies. Some of them even went out of their way to be robbed by him! A number of somewhat besotted gentlewomen almost saved his life by petitioning the King and other members of the government, stressing that Duval had never killed or harmed a soul, he had merely embarrassed one or two fellows who could afford to lose some of their excessive wealth. The ladies almost succeeded; the King, the younger Charles, who as you may recall was putty in the hands of pretty women, is said to have admired Duval, but left the matter to a damnable judge who would hear nothing of a reprieve. On the day of his execution a waft of wealthy women, some of them Duval's victims, others just eager to catch a glimpse of the devilishly handsome fellow, were at Tyburn gallows. Some even released white doves as a symbol of their sorrow. Many tender hearts were broken that day and many hot tears were shed, with a myriad of damp cheeks beneath dark veils. Notwithstanding the distress of their wives, daughters or even mothers, many men were secretly relieved that this thief of property and passions, was no more.

So, while I longed to be a legend and achieve immortality and cause palpitations and an outbreak of female hysteria, I felt that my death was far too big a price to pay. That said, it was a brutal time and so my reckoning was that I may as well be hanged for a sheep as a lamb, or more accurately a purse of silver and gold, or a necklace still warm from the breast of a beautiful woman. I just needed to be careful as with every theft, and particularly where there was a need to dispose of jewellery or other items, there was a risk that someone willingly or wantonly would reveal my identity. In fact, disposing of the proceeds of my robberies was often more difficult than the actual crime and needed special treatment.

It was somewhat ironic that amongst the spew of lawyers around Temple, there was the most villainous public house in London. The Devil Tavern. A place where everything imaginable, and some things best consigned to nightmares, could be bought, and sold. It was a place where every pair of eyes, seemed to observe <u>all</u> movements and every ear listened attentively to <u>all</u> conversation. The place seemed full of owls each hunting in the half-light. But the only way to survive, to sell my spoils, was to befriend these creatures of the twilight.

But one can only stay close to predators for so long, and there would come a time when their unblinking eyes would turn towards you, and gaze for too-long a moment. They would be unable to control their destructive impulses. They would devour their young, their kin, or anyone else in their flight who had served their purpose or was the victim of a wicked whim. I needed to leave this damnable place behind before I felt the fatal pressure of pin sharp claws, or fell prey to their tattling.

The Bow Street Runners began to publish increasingly accurate reports of my misdemeanours in the newspapers, complete with details of some of the more noticeable stolen items. The main roads into London were now patrolled by well-armed, thick-set men. The net was tightening. I tried to go back to painting but with every month more and more skilled men were drawn to London where they were chasing fewer jobs. The world was in turmoil, some of the banks had ceased trading taking with them the money of those fools who believed the never-ending lie about easy money and fast profits. As always those who suffered most were the poor; panic caused prices, even for the staples of bread, cheese, meat, and ale to rise beyond the reach of many. The banks killed, albeit indirectly, thousands of those less able to cope. Murdered by the greed of others. While many of the poor folk who stole to live found their way to Newgate's tight embrace, I never saw a single banker on the gallows!

Just one more thing before I leave behind my highwayman days. When you travel you collect stories. Ancient roads tell the most tales. The Great North Road is a library of legend. One story told to me when I stayed close by the Holy Island of Lindisfarne was of Grizel Cochrane, who when she was only 19 years old dressed as a man to hold up the mail coach from London which was carrying her father's death warrant. She seized and destroyed the document. The ensuing delay gave her father enough time to obtain a royal pardon. A lovely story of daughterly love and derring-do which I forgot until a year or so later when I stopped a coach, the spoils of which included a packet with a Royal seal. In it was some confidential, if dull, correspondence, as well as a death warrant for a member of the nobility. Sensing an opportunity to make money as well as save a life, I considered presenting myself to the gentleman concerned offering him the document in return for gold. My enquiries however concluded that he – in common with many of his class - was a rogue who would no doubt seize and destroy the document, therefore ensuring his safety at least for a while, before turning me in and seeing me hanged for robbery. I burned the warrant and left the gentleman to his own fate.

Each dawn would see the arrest of more of my confederates. There were tales of The Runners offering rewards and bribes to free the tongue. In those hard times increasingly, no one could be trusted. London was rapidly becoming far too dangerous a place. It became yet more perilous for me when I intervened in a dispute between a master and servant. The latter had been beaten to within an inch of his life for what it transpired was a very minor transgression. His master's pistol had struck his face repeatedly, bone was exposed and the black lad's eye was loose in its socket. In the London manner, a crowd had gathered to watch but not intervene. With no time to think, I waded in removing the bully and casting him and his pistol to the dirt. He cursed my back as I guided the injured youngster to the surgery of the kindly Doctor Sharp.

The bully was the winning combination of plantation owner and lawyer. He sought revenge and promised to pay The Runners a tidy sum if they apprehended the Scottish ruffian who unprovoked – his words as recorded in the press - had attacked him as he went *about his business in the street. Now more than ever, I needed to leave. My mind went back to the cold pews of Greyfriar's Church, to Reverend Erskine's sermons and his tales of a new world and a new life."*

Jack's voice had become a whisper, he was visibly tired by his memories.

"Friend, I have spoken enough" he said, *"please tell me more of your own story."*

Chapter Six

I cast my mind back to my own far-off land.

It was a bright spring day with an azure sky flecked with coral-coloured creamy wisps of cloud. A beautiful day for a wedding. Cars and trucks arrived each with their own celebratory plume of dust, and scrunch of tyres on gravel, before they disgorged their cargoes of jolly guests. The white-painted, iridescent venue was bedecked with bright bunting which flickered, and licked its little tongues in the wind. There was joy on many faces although the groom was visibly – even from my eyrie - a pensive bundle of nerves. All filed inside for the ceremony, the Nikah. There was gaiety and laughter minutes later when the guests and the wedded couple filed into open air. On the roof of the adjoining building a handful of guests were firing their guns at the sky, sun-caught bullet casing confetti rained down.

My radio crackled. "Target, gold turban, by blue Toyota pickup" was Phil's terse message. I confirmed the target.

Larry shot straight and true, gold began to run red. Once again as Hiawatha, swifter flew my second "arrow," in the pathway of the former, piercing deeper than the other in the white of the target's shirt, wounding sorer than its brother. The target's knees trembled like windy reeds beneath him before he bent and crumpled to the floor. Then for one split second, an infinitesimally small period of time, I saw the target gaze straight at me, from one side of the valley right to the other, he looked straight down the telescopic sight, into my eye, my heart, my soul. I do not know who he saw at that precise instant, when I took his life, whether it was Allah or Satan. But I saw a wedding day, the happiest day of a couple's life, destroyed.

My thoughts flitted back to Valerie's and my own special day, the flowers, the smiles, the colours, the choir, the music, the sheer unadulterated joy.

My eyes moistened, dust obviously.

"Target down, kill confirmed." Phil's terse tones brought me back to the present. I took one last look; I wish to this day that I had not. The bride, whose father I had just killed, cradled, and comforted him. Her beautiful, bright bridal gown was soaked with blood, with gore and with the tears that fell from her anguished face. The seconds it took for me to decamp and slide from the mountain seemed like hours. My eyes were full of stone, sand, and sky as I, and then we, trekked the miles to our pick-up point. But my minds-eye was full of another day, many miles to the west, a day when a bumbling but good-natured vicar forgot, until prompted by the verger, to ask if anyone knew of any "cause or just impediment why these persons should not be joined together in Holy Matrimony." A wedding where my heart fluttered like a caged bird and there was a tear of joy in my eye throughout. A wedding where my Valerie was the most beautiful woman I had ever seen. A wedding where the choir and congregation sang, and angels appeared to join in with them. Our day had been beautiful. Although I did not know it at the time, we would never be happier.

And here I was, in a country where no one would ever love us, having obeyed an order to kill a man on his proudest, and his daughter's happiest, day.

The moment a body falls dead – no matter how violent their demise – there is an instant when they drift slowly downward like an autumn leaf, as though at last they are weightless and free. When you see your first victim fall, Death itself then begins to possess you. It begins with the ears, your hearing becomes dulled. Your eyes become covered, veiled. Your mouth is muffled. Your heart hardens, so you cannot resist the dark which is laid upon you. Death will not brook resistance, Death silences dissent, Death is the despotic puppeteer.

That night back at base, I cradled Valerie's letters with their wonderful tumble of words made more musical by her handwriting which curled like new-born ferns. Her letters which made the desert bloom. I held the paper to my face, I inhaled my darling's perfume, I re-read, I then wept."

As I shared my story with Jack, I wept once more.

"There had been many days, and many missions when what I did felt right, when I had purpose. The days when we saw a country rebuilding, schools, hospitals, roads, lives. But there were others when I saw my colleagues under fire, when I saw the dirt, the muck, the grit, the grime, and gore of war, where once friendly smiles flamed into hate, and the everyday – cars, luggage, shopping – were transformed, demonised.

One morning on patrol we came across a discarded fridge, lying broken and exhausted, apparently stripped of anything of value. It was probably an empty shell, but like a bad mussel its mouth was shut tight. In Afghan you learn that no act is a coincidence, even the simple closing of a door. Where the compressor had been, was now a new black clam shell. Something far too new, and too clean for this second-hand country, where everything – politics, people, houses, cars, history, and peace - was gaffer taped together. We radioed in reporting a suspected IED – an improvised explosive device – and requested a bomb disposal crew. Whilst waiting for the Bomb Squad we hung back, twenty, thirty yards away from the fridge, picking our way backwards, boots tiptoeing, seeking whatever shelter we could find. The invisible bomber then blew.

In the aftermath of splintered steel and shrapnel the devils revealed themselves, rising from the dust. I rose, shot, ran, and fired again and again to try to save my colleagues, as well as the poor unfortunate civilians whose only crime was to have been born at the wrong time, under the wrong broad, blue impassive sky and on this piece of earth where men and minds melt. There were many days like this.

It is my belief that with each breath we inhale an infinitesimally small part of those around us, as well as sharing a tiny part of the very fabric of our own life with others. The air around us is full of microscopic particles of the living and the dead. I am sure that with every death I caused, not only did a small part of me die, but that I absorbed a tiny fraction of those I killed, as though their need to live on became a starburst meshing with all those around them. Perhaps this is the reason every sniper has a limited time before he, and it is nearly always he, is unable to be fully himself. They have been too close, they have seen too much, too vividly. Every shot leaves a blood splatter and an imprint. I do not know how others feel or felt, but I know that I began to fear sleep as the shadows which are at the corners of our eyes in the day began to come close, clawing, screaming in the depths of night.

And another thing, during my days in Afghan – we never gave it its full name, we all felt that two syllables was more than enough for that weary land – was that I learned to hate sand. Previously the feeling of the tiny granules between my toes had been joyful, accompanied as they usually were by squeals of laughter, ice cream, beach cricket, ambitious hungry seagulls, dozing grandmothers, the ice-cold North Sea and the fragrance of fish and chips. Sand was now in, between and among everything we owned, every orifice was sand blasted, a constant reminder that even the land itself despised us."

Tear stained and yet more crumpled, I continued.

"There are many reasons I am now here by the sea, loveless, and homeless. I am the sum of all my disappointments and regrets. I have known love, but, I have stupidly, thoughtlessly, spurned it. I should have shown my Mam so much more love than I ever did. The world turns while taking and giving life. In a hospital on a hill in a quiet room, her arms pierced with tubes, her face masked, her hands held by her besotted husband, Mam died.

I should have been with her when she passed, but war does not wait. We had spoken a few days before, me in a corner of camp, her on the telephone which wheels its way from ward to ward. Me moaning, complaining, and cursing, she listening, loving, calming, both of us all the while racked with the pain of the present and knowledge that her future was almost finished. I did not sense her terror in our final phone call. When I think of it now, I remember the gaps between words which was so unlike Mam who usually spoke in a sparrow like chatter. Poor description. Not a sparrow; her speech was more beautiful than that, she lilted and sang like a lark. Those gaps I later realised, had grown over time, where regular breaths had once been were now hard intakes of air fighting to gain entry to her shrivelling lungs.

At first Dad kept himself busy, the garden which had been neglected during the years when he lovingly cared for his darling wife, once again became his joy. It soon blossomed: roses, tended with the annual tractor load of manure; hydrangeas and geraniums in the front; vegetables round the back. At the end of every visit, we would leave with an armful of produce, and let me tell you nothing ever tasted better than Dad's home-grown potatoes…

It is the small things that bring back so much.

Dad re-joined a choir he had been a member of as a young man. His brandy-like voice would rise above and sweep around the others. They played some concerts in village halls, churches and one at the Cathedral where I had the honour to be among the audience. The tenors and basses were blazered and shiny-shoed;

they were wonderful. Science may disagree with me, but, I feel, no I know, that there is some music which makes the stones themselves dance, and Cuthbert's ancient shrine cavorted that night.

One of the Choir's songs was the spiritual "There is a balm in Gilead," when they sang it that night the music snaked upwards towards the stained-glass windows which I swear shone brighter. I have never truly thought about the lyrics until this very moment:

"There is a balm in Gilead
To make the wounded whole;
There's power in heaven,
To cure a sin-sick soul."

I now think I know that when Dad sang that song way back then, he was giving me a memory to call upon when the dark dog walked by my side.

For a couple of years after Mam's passing, he held his grief at bay, distraction working for a while. Then two things happened close to one another - a pan left on a hob and the choir closing. The first set off a fire alarm which was heard and responded to by a kindly neighbour. The latter was reported as 'The ink drying on the last chapter' by the local paper punning on the Choir's colliery heritage. Dad could no longer be left alone, and his singing had been taken from him. Many rooms that you have when you are younger become locked as you grow old. He moved from the family home with the garden he had once again grown to love into sheltered accommodation, then to a place where he had one small room, and a sub-tropical communal space which was dominated by a television which numbed everything before it, a cathode opiate.

His memory, once pin sharp, became blunted. Our conversations would always loop "Where are you living now?" "How long are you up for?" "What are you doing now?" "When are you going?" "How long have I been here?" and, with the permanent twinkle in his eye "Is this your new girlfriend?" which he would squirmingly ask whenever I took Valerie with me. He had been at the wedding where he had sung so beautifully in church, and danced the night away at the reception. But he now had no memory of that day or any other in the last twenty or so years. Ten minutes later the same sequence of questions. Although I despised the illness that had robbed him of much, I learned to - eventually - love the gentleness that it brought.

Whenever I returned on leave, I would of course visit him. We would talk about music, the books I had brought him – my love of books came from Dad, no Saturday shopping trip was complete for him unless he returned with a handful from a charity shop. To try to avoid some of the inevitable repetition, we would try to find a quiet corner, sometimes - North Eastern weather permitting - outside in the sun-lit courtyard, and I would read to him. A chapter of a Dennis Wheatley novel, or an M.R. James ghost story were his favourites; he had always been a fan of the ghoulish. We once went to see the blood-soaked Sondheim opera Sweeney Todd in Newcastle. I think I was only twelve, and we were in the front row! I have seen so much bloodshed since, but the glint of Sweeney's razor still fills me with dread.

He had served with the Royal Engineers but had not seen combat, and for that he always counted his blessings. Among the loop of questions two new ones emerged, "How is it?" and a stumbling "How are you?" I guess that he had seen the television news and the succession of draped coffins delivered by Hercules. The final labour.

"Oh, I'm alright Dad, they'll never get me." I would say, bravado squeaking from every pore, trying to believe it myself. He would squeeze my hand, his fat fingers, surprisingly dextrous when placed on a piano, wrapping around mine. "You're not a small target mind" his sense of humour undimmed, but pots and kettles...

I was told my Dad was slipping away in a call I received from my brother. Dad had been in and out of hospital for the last five or so years. Each time we felt that it might be the last but he would bounce back. My brother's usually inexpressive voice was wracked with emotion, "but, this time..."

But once again I could not return. I was too far away and just about to be deployed on an operation that was too important to abort or re-schedule, I recorded a message for my brother to play to Dad. I told him to perk up, sang him a verse of something - he always joked that I did not need to shoot the enemy, just sing to them - and told him I would bring him a bottle of something very special back when I came home. He was a very occasional drinker, but he did love single malt whiskies, the smokier the better. Between us we had polished off a few bottles over the years, more recently surreptitiously around his bedside or in his tiny room while the nursing home staff intentionally looked the other way.

He died a week after my brother's call, my brother and sisters around his bed, while I, his firstborn son, was on a killing mission.

On my return to camp my commanding officer ushered me into what passes for an office when the walls are canvas. "I'm sorry" he said. "We can fly you back…" I stopped him. My Dad had died and was now buried, and there was nothing for me to do. I thanked him and left, then sought out a quiet corner to try to talk to Dad, but I could not; the words failed me. I had lost the chance to say goodbye to both of my parents. The night sky above my head was clear, my mind was not."

Jack's gaze dropped. His voice quiet. *"When they are gone it as though the buttresses which have supported you are swept away, your wall must now stand alone. The broken stones which lie scattered around us are the memories, some of which are disconnected, bruised. But they are still there no matter how long the grass."*

He gave a wan smile which I sensed offered me a chance to stop for a while, but I needed to continue.

"So, with each death I pray that I am saving people from the twenty first century fever of intolerance. The irony is not lost on me. In Afghan we hoped that we were building safe places where girls could go to school, hospitals to treat the sick, and fertile fields where crops, not just the ubiquitous poppy, could be grown. We thought we were building a nation, we told ourselves we were making this place better for everyone. We even hoped that eventually those who we fought would see that peace was the best of all possible worlds. The lads who had served in Northern Ireland held that hope perhaps the dearest of all of us.

My killings became less an act of heroism, and more a ritual slaughter. I lost count of, or more truthfully tried to forget, the number I killed. It was well short of the 496 German soldiers whose lives were ended by Nikolay Yakovlevich Ilyin at Stalingrad, but every few weeks I edged closer. Although in the preparation for, and during the mission itself I was professionalism personified, afterwards, I immediately expunged, cleansed, and scrubbed my mind of the deed. At least I tried to, but like an actor who deletes lines of a delivered play to create space for the next role, there are some words and phrases that snag and stay, some images you are unable to forget. So like an actor I wore a mental mask; increasingly one of tragedy.

My skin physically hardened, but instead of keeping out slings and arrows, it kept them in, so that they became my own torture, my own iron maiden, my pain permanent yet invisible. Into my brain were burned the sight of sand-scattered dead men on hillsides, in ditches, cars, and buildings. No longer exceptional, death had now become monotonous, but never forgettable.

Gradually my face too became an impassive mask, with my personality driven out. My eyes always half closed as though to keep the horrors out, with my lips a thin line, some disappearing horizon. Set firm."

Jack shook his head ever-so slightly. *"But life paints masks on us all Will."* My thoughts and words surged. "But my greatest regret is <u>not</u> to have killed. As you mentioned an hour or two ago, I have lost track of time, I failed to complete one mission. I had the target in my sights, but clinging to his legs were his two or three year old daughter. Her eyes bright, hair wind-blown, smile wide, beauty and joy. I could not take away her father. I deliberately waited too long, for others to come onto the scene, for the shot to be compromised, to be unsafe. I then had good cause not to proceed, but I knew the truth. I had failed."

"On Sunday in a wind-tossed tent, those of us who could would gather for the rather ramshackle weekly service. An unconvincing balding blonde haired parson, straight from a Two Ronnies' sketch, sought to sooth and save, spouting platitudes and scripture. His sermons were littered with academic references, as though he needed to convince us that his words had weight. For the most part we had no idea whether the theology was sound, and to be honest we did not care. Most of us knew little religion, apart from weddings, christenings (sometimes in that order), and the occasional post-pub Christmas Eve singalong that passed for the midnight service we were dragged along to by more faithful family members.

My sisters, my brother and I were peripatetic parishioners. We sampled the range of Sunday morning services our small village had to offer. From Methodist Hall to Salvation Army Citadel, to the happy-clappy church in the library (whose name I cannot remember but was probably something to do with new something or other) and to the sedation of the blue-rinsed Anglican Church. We never settled on one, and as neither parent truly cared for faith, something I now regret not understanding, we were never pushed.

In the tent the chaplain would lead our mumbling and self-conscious unaccompanied singing. We would then pray, audibly for the Queen, our leaders, our communities, for our forces overseas, for countries at war, for our fallen, for our families and for us. There would then be a time for silent prayer which was never long enough to penetrate our hardened hearts and release the intensity of emotion, anguish and fear that lay buried there. The crack of the communion wafer, the gulps of wine and the hurried "Amens," were a soundtrack to something we would never dream of missing, but which never lit a Godly fire.

Between services the chaplain hid himself away, the Hermit of Helmand we called him. He was praying, always praying; something I never did, or really tried until I went to Afghan. It is something I still do not, and perhaps will never fully understand, but it has never stopped me from trying. There is one particular prayer I keep coming back to time and again, it is the one given to me by my chapel going Aunt. She had written it on a slip of paper, she would be so pleased to know that back then it went with me everywhere.

"God keep my mind and body clean,
and save my soul from growing mean.
God help me fight outside and in
the deadly foes of self and sin.
God bless those near and dear to me.
And keep us loyal and true to thee.
God help us all to put to rout
Those enemies of distrust and doubt.
God give me when by sin enticed
The courage and power of Jesus Christ."

The more evil I saw in the world the more I wanted to believe in good, God, or at least something better."

The streets were now quiet, the neon lights had dimmed, the revellers had returned home. Jack and I were almost alone, with our stories and the sea.

Chapter Seven

Although I had spoken for some time, I did not yet want to pause and hear more of Jack's tale; my own story pulled at its own lead.

"Then there was the day, in everyone's life there is THE DAY, every minute of which is snagged on a barb of your memory. My own began in a non-descript way, with a breakfast even Oliver Twist would have turned his nose up at, followed by a briefing on the day's mission. Phil and I had been back at base for a while and were taking our turn with fellow soldiers on routine patrols across this Looking Glass of a country, where everything was other.

Today, we were in a residential area to conduct a community reassurance patrol. We told ourselves we were providing encouragement to, and giving hope to the Afghan population. But a country which only fifteen or so years ago was in the chaos and carnage of civil war, with the troops of another superpower on its streets, needs a great deal of bolstering. There were the ubiquitous blast walls which seemed to grab shadows out of the air, checkpoints everywhere, and ever-circling vulture-like helicopters. But how can you truly reassure a people when they know that you, just like every other nation which has set foot in this country, will eventually disappear? The Afghan people do not like foreigners in their land. They may hate each other, but they hate outsiders far more. That, coupled with ties which are strong and transmitted from one generation to the next and from uncle to nephew to cousin, means there is a web more complex than any made with server and wire. The mujahideen, and the Taliban know every bush and gully of this land, they can live off its – to us – invisible bounty; they even wipe their arses on its stones for heaven's sake!

I am usually okay for people to practice whatever religion suits them, provided – as I mentioned earlier - they don't knock on my front door early on a weekend morning, but the Taliban, they are strange ones. Apparently, the word itself means student, yet they are opposed to every type of art; they smashed the ancient statues of the National Museum in Kabul destroying Zeus and Buddha with hundreds of hammers. They even banned music! What sort of ideology has no place for song? As a wise Welshman once said to me "Wonderful is a world that sings, gentle are its songs." But Afghan was the opposite of a gentle world; there seemed to be tears and sobs in every wall, zealots were everywhere, and sadly, they were in every colour uniform, not just those of the enemy. Fanatics will be the end of us all.

A short ride in an armoured personnel carrier with the suspension of a sports car, but none of the appeal, was followed by a twitchy twenty-minute, sweat-soaked walk. It was another normal street, fly blown, and litter strewn. That was one of the things that first leaped at me about Afghan – the litter! It is a land where white plastic bags flock in their thousands, blown by the slightest breath of wind, rushing hither and yon, like miniature ghosts playing schoolyard football. One of my many opinions was that this place needed a spring clean organised by the local Women's Institute. It required a squadron of long handled litter pickers, a battalion of daffodil coloured Marigold gloves, a barrage of black plastic bags, and a platoon of couples called Simon and Judie, fuelled by a sense of indignation, tea, Marks & Spencer biscuits, and the desire to post something on Instagram."

Not for the first time Jack's expression indicated he did not fully understand, but there was no time for explanation.

"Amongst the wind-blown waste was a football. It was orange with faded black lettering, panelled with a suggestion that it had once been round, it was scuffed like a year-old pair of school shoes. Phil had told me many times about his skill as a junior footballer; he played for the school, then the county. He was scouted by a number of Scottish teams who saw his potential. We all have our litany of missed opportunities and roads not travelled, but with Phil there was more truth than most.

But as a young man he wasn't excited at the prospect of turning professional, he only saw a less than heady cocktail of uncertainty and drudgery; he saw twenty years or more mapped out in away fixtures at Forfar. "Nah, I wanted to enjoy my football, I never wanted to be famous and have my name sung by thousands of strangers, I just wanted an anonymous, enjoyable, normal life you know..." The unsaid was that the life he, I, and everyone around us was living was far from ordinary.

But life deals cards, sometimes from the bottom of the deck, and sometimes marked. The truth was he and I were still not too sure we knew what we wanted to be when we grew up. They say there is a very fine line between philosophy and soldiering. Both seek the meaning of life, one through thought and the other through deeds. When you are away from home, you think of nothing else but your meaning, purpose, and those you are defending. My bride and our bump were my first thought on waking, and my final prayer before sleeping. The nightmare was coming to an end, it would soon be over, just one month more. Phil and I had joined up at the same time, eight years ago, we served our minimum time and then signed on for more, hoping that things would only get better. They hadn't. We had both decided to go back to civvy street.

An army barracks in a hostile country is a prison. You are allowed out for heavily armoured patrols once a day, more if you are "lucky." You do your share of guard duty. You clean and re-clean your weapons, as you never know when your life will depend on them. You rest and attempt to picture yourself elsewhere. Some of the lads had instruments, and there is usually a battered acoustic guitar being strangled in a corner somewhere with the dying gasps of some popular song. Sometimes others would join in to – depending on your perspective - drown out or add to the cacophony. One second lieutenant seemed to be on a personal mission to convince the British Army that the oboe is a weapon of war. There were banjo players, harmonica-ists and then me on bones, the smoothed pieces of wood that click and clack. Most of the songs we would demolish were well known, lubricating the mix of ages and backgrounds, but some were more than that, they were statements of identity. Many were folk songs, wistful tales from high Scottish hills, singalong anthems about Yorkshire Moors or from seafaring towns tales of sunken ships and drowned love. The father of one of the lads from Portsmouth had written and recorded a few songs which his proud son would play to us when we couldn't cope with another Oasis, Beatles, or Blur number. With due respect to this lad's dad, a fellow called Brian Hooper, they were mostly forgettable, but there was one which grabbed us, perhaps because of its tale of justice being meted out to a villain, or its reference to a drunken pub crawl. In Afghan we were always thirsty. Anyhow, and I can't believe I am really saying this, but Jack, the song was about you.

"At the mouth of Portsmouth Harbour, where the old chain ferry plied,
Some say a spirit hangs in chains where submarines now glide.
Though his bones have gone, the Devil knows where,
Jack the Painter lingers there.
Now Painter Jack's just bones in a sack, but the Dockyard's working yet.

Though Jack, he was a painter, as a brand he made his name:
He met his fate in Portsmouth, where he set the 'Yard aflame.
But the firemen bold and the seaman brave doused the flames, the fleet to save:
Now Painter Jack's just bones in a sack, but the Dockyard's working yet.

At Winchester the trial was held and the sentence it was passed;

Jack hanged at the gate of the Dockyard from the Arethusa's
mast.
Though the rope store stood a blackened wreck,
There was rope enough for the Painter's neck:
Now Painter Jack's just bones in a sack, but the Dockyard's
working yet.

In chains he hung at Blockhouse Point, and stayed for many
a year,
'til taken to an alehouse as a pledge to pay for beer.
So, if you've no money, just a body in a sack,
You can try for a drink on Painter Jack:
Now Painter Jack's just bones in a sack, but the Dockyard's
working yet."

So you see Jack, I knew some of your story even before you
began to tell it. But from what you say that song doesn't give
the full picture now does it?"

"Well it's not every day you hear a song about a painter." My new
friend tried to lighten the mood. I actually knew of quite a few
but I didn't interrupt; it wasn't the time. *"No, it doesn't tell the
full story. History, they say, is always written by the victors, very
rarely by the likes of us."* We both shook our heads, we knew
our place. *"I never had much time for song."* Once again Jack
was deep in his memories. "But I, and many of my comrades
did, and music was a balm for us. Particularly those songs
which come from the borderlands, that place where song, hope,
dread, love, and fear reside. One such song "December" by the
Waterboys became an anthem for us:

"December is the cruellest month
this time for once my cheeks are warm.
After long years in the monkey-house
I am ready for the storm.
Let them throw all their cannonballs.
Let all their strongmen come.
I'm ready to go anywhere
through venom, sick and scum!"

We were in the "anywhere," we were in the eye of the "storm," where the strongmen came in waves. In the distant desert we felt alone and sometimes, betrayed. When not a target for our human enemy, we were food for sand flies and mosquitoes and surrounded by shade seeking scorpions who loved army boots most of all. Politician after politician – when they discovered peace was an easy promise but an impossible reality - washed their hands of us. Austerity came and the social contract – the promise of the state to look after its armed forces - was broken as easily as any other Tory promise. Our future was gambled away like a crucifixion cloak.

In addition to song, another distraction was the Sunday kick about, which was usually after the church service, and before the hallowed roast dinner which wouldn't have earned that description in my family. There were never any proper Yorkshire puddings, the caramel-coloured pillows of gravy-soaked perfection, which in our house went with every Sunday roast. We had the misfortune to have southerners in the kitchen, and it wasn't their fault that they had never before experienced the magic which can be made with just eggs, milk and flour. Their attempts were always flat, greasy, and burned. I was tempted to give up on them and have something else instead, but I didn't, there was always hope that the cookhouse would one day appoint a northern chef.

I have a tendency to digress. Excuse me Jack. Anyway, back to the football. Perhaps Phil mistook the raddled backstreet for green sward. Every single second of what follows is etched, branded on my mind. His boyish, lopsided grin. The way he ran from the path, the creak of his body armour, and the swirl of dust. It happened so quickly we could not react, apart from the commanding officer who barked "Jesus suffering fuck, what are you doing man?"

Phil's leg bent back, his foot arched, his incomplete cry of "Goal!"

The earth rose and the sky fell. It was one of those moments where time itself seems to fork and fracture, where phantom lives speed like shooting stars before crashing, cratered, crevassed.

There is an intensity, almost a purity to extreme pain. I have so far suffered it once, and I never wish to endure it again. I am told that I was thrown into the air, my helmet and Kevlar vest took the brunt of the blast. Ball bearings rained down, things we used to play with, as marbles, as children, were terrorised in Afghan. I landed twisted. Bullets flew around me and the others, some of my comrades were crawling, some were running, but some were incapable of either. I was blessed that a quick thinking, fast talking Scouser spotted a wheelbarrow and pushed me like a prize marrow behind a wall, I was sheltered until help eventually came."

Jack looked towards, then through me. *"You were lucky."*

My mind re-misted "Luck?!" I roared as the sea clawed at the pebbles below.

"I'm sorry" there was a hint of Jack's stutter *"my words sometimes escape before they are ready."* A few minutes, then a few more passed, before I was calm enough to speak.

Chapter Eight

Jack's word "*lucky*" still burned in my ears. He was wrong, I needed to explain, so my story continued.

"I was told all of this when I woke up some days later, initially to a bright blur, the air cool, calm, and clean, awash with birdsong.

Moments later there was a bustle, a fresh-faced nurse entered filling the room with a bright welcoming, singsong "Good morning."

Three of us ended up in adjoining beds. Kieran a noisy Welshman with an arm that would never again throw darts. Me with no flesh below one knee and no right arm. Phil with no legs, and the rest of his body raked by nuts, ball bearings, bolts, and nails.

He had once told me that when he went, he would like me to take charge of his funeral, and that what he wished for most of all was a sky burial, to be mounted on an excarnation platform where the eagles, buzzards and crows would strip his flesh and keep it in the thin air where he thought he belonged. "Why that's going to look a bit daft in Stirling High Street, and I'm not too sure the Coop Funeral Services do that sort of thing." was my considered reply. His wish had half come true, much of his body had already been scattered to the four winds.

Over the next days and weeks thoughts flitted by, landing for a moment before dashing off to where they were meant to be. Some stayed for longer, memories that must have convinced the nurses that they needed to be allowed to visit. Snippets from books, songs, poems, and conversations all came and went. It was the books which came back to me most vividly. As a youth I would read voraciously in the clear light of the top deck of the number 721 bus to Newcastle. Back then, I devoured and was powered by words. I would read books I understood: thrillers, comedies, those at the edges of other worlds, stories of epic travel which took me from the backstreets of my smoky former pit village to the Hindu Kush, The Apennines of Italy, or the magical Songlines of Australia. There were those other books which made my mind sore, I read them because they challenged me, and I was not someone to back down, in that way I was very much my father's son.

One book, on the subject of mankind's development by Margaret Mead argued that the first sign of civilisation was not fishhooks, weapons, or pottery but a broken femur that had healed. If an animal breaks a leg it dies of starvation or is prey for wild beasts, it does not survive long enough for the bone to heal. I recall that Mead's book said something to the effect that "A broken femur that has healed is evidence that someone has stayed with the one who fell, has bound the wound, carried them to safety and tended them until they recovered. Helping someone else through difficulty is where civilisation starts."

Here I was surrounded by those who lives are spent staying with, binding, carrying, and tending others.

Between our morphine trips as our pain subsided, we spoke of all the things we would do when we were discharged. Kieran would work in his Dad's garage restoring vintage cars to glory, I was to cradle my daughter and show her the beauty of the world, and Phil would pull himself together (his words) and climb Everest. Aye, he still harboured that dream, even then. I never shed so many hidden tears than when he mentioned the mountain.

It was three o'clock, outside the world was asleep, but by our beds there was a kerfuffle, a shuffle of feet, a stuttering rumble of approaching equipment, wheels clicking. There was the whisper and sigh of gases being connected. There was the muffled firework like sound of defibrillators. Behind the inadequate blue fabric screens, there were countless medical staff, and frantic activity. At first there was much said, but gradually there were fewer more intense words.

The two electronic notes, which told a simple song of life, lost their melody and one of their number. In that small intimate corner of the world everyone was awake, we all prayed, hope against hope for the second note to return. But no, at that instant, something tangible left all of us. There were straight-line mouths, hushed words, and misted eyes. There was less, we were all less.

Phil's life was over.

From that moment, when I heard the single plaintive note, there has been a shadow across my heart."

My eyes were full.

Jack shook his head in shared sorrow.

Chapter Nine

"The hospital now felt empty, cavernous, it had become a place of shadows. Phil had gone, my companion, my soul mate, my conscience, my guide was no more. Although his bed was soon filled by another broken soul, the space remained empty.

I was surrounded by comrades with legs and arms missing, their stumps like newly split figs, their wounds red candle wax, forever angry with a sliver of dark oily smoke. Young men who would never again be whole, missing pounds of flesh, settlement of some unholy Shakespearean debt, paying for the sins of others, forever earthbound. The Bard's Lear observed "As flies to wanton boys are we to the gods, they kill us for their sport." There are far too many rulers who believe themselves to be gods and there is too much sport in this godforsaken world.

Some comrades (physically) healed and left; others departed.

Although I excelled in the Army, I always felt a fraud, surrounded by those with more skill, commitment, and discipline than I could ever hope to have. It was luck combined with serendipity that had moved me along and helped me be recognised. I never really thought about how fickle fate was until the night Phil passed on, when a real soldier had been taken, whilst the fraud in the next bed still lived. Why him and not me? Why?

Some days later, I learned that the bombmaker responsible for the devices which had killed Phil and many others had been captured. I knew his name. I knew his face. I would never forget what I should have done, and the many lives which would have been saved had I done my duty.

Each night I would turn towards the window and curse the darkness and, in the morning I would curse the light which I did not deserve.

But whatever horrors I had seen, whatever pain was now etched upon every cell of my incomplete body, there would always be Valerie. Her eyes were the very first things I noticed in the fixed spotlight of a makeshift stage, bright bold blue, gentle yet strong, a whole delightful world encased in a seam of kohl. "Your eyes" I said, "Reach me a gentian, give me a torch! Let me guide myself with the blue, forked torch of this flower."

An embodiment of cool, even she was momentarily taken aback. I suppose she was expecting some lager-soaked line about me needing a map because I was lost in her eyes. But I was never good at that sort of chat. "Ah, a drummer who likes poetry." At that point she did not know it was one of the very few lines I did know. Grandma's favourite flowers were gentians which Grandad of course grew in their small back garden, that was where he taught me the DH Lawrence poem. Valerie smiled her wonderful sunrise of a smile, her cheekbones sharpened, her nose wrinkled and wriggled ever so slightly, her lips curled as an as yet unnamed punctuation mark, those eyes sparkled, and the world was filled with light.

I was on leave and earlier that day had caught up with one

of my old band mates. They were playing that night at The George, and guitarist Peter had asked if I would play a couple of songs with them. Having not played for a couple of years I was as rusty as hell, but it was a gig, so of course I agreed. The band were good, probably better without me; their usual drummer was rock steady, none of the speeding up and attempted jazz-fills of yours truly. The pub was pretty full and in a good mood. One or two of the long-term fans, once they had seen through the severe haircut, and deep tan, recognised me. Before the intermission I was invited up onto the tiny stage, and we immediately launched into a version of The Surfaris' "Wipe Out." It was a chance for me to improvise and show how good, bad, or indifferent a drummer I really was. The toms thundered and rolled. The song slowed and sped like a cornering rally car with my arms flailing octopus like around the cymbals, snare, drums, rims, and whatever was in reach. The music slowed right down to just a pulse, a hint of a bass drum, a low-level hibernating heartbeat, before building into a frenzy with the crowd belting out the "Na, na, na, na, na, na, nah" melody. We then went into a medley of snatches of other songs: the Who's "Magic Bus," Buffalo Springfield's "For what it's worth," Roxy's "Virginia Plain," before ending with Lindisfarne's "Fog on the Tyne" which was a sort of anthem for thereabouts, even for those of us who would never, ever go to Newcastle on a match day. All and sundry sang the entire song, taking great pleasure in Alan Hull's genius alliteration "Sittin' in a sleazy snack-bar suckin' sickly sausage rolls, slippin' down slowly, slippin' down sideways. Think I'll sign off the dole." We eventually stopped, in a fug of happiness, contentment and raging thirst which presaged a mass exodus to the bar which was led by the singer and guitarist. My arms were aching, it had been too, too long since I had sat behind a kit. I had once been a contender, a hopeful, I was now merely hopeful that some kind soul would buy me a pint.

The two vocal microphones were unoccupied. In the blink of an eye, one wasn't and from it came swaying a voice of smoke.

"I hear the sound" whatever hubbub there was around the bar stopped, "of distant" pause "drums." The last phrase was a question to me. I replied with a shimmer of cymbals before the malleted slow pum, pa-ba rhythm. The song was carried forward by just the two of us, the stranger swayed like a sapling in a summer breeze, her voice, Valerie's voice, needing no accompaniment apart from my own.

We fell in love, the wonderful all-encompassing sense that you, like a caterpillar emerging from its cocoon to become a butterfly have found your bright, light, joyous, fluttering twin; you no longer dance alone, each step has an echo. You hold and are held. You no longer fall. Joy has become your act of resistance.

While I was in hospital Valerie gave birth to our daughter. I felt joy tinged with sadness, another place I had not been when I was needed."

Jack looked wistful, "*I never knew romantic love, passion yes, but that very soon fades. Indeed, I wish I had truly cherished someone and been loved in return, but young men do not always see or recognise that which is most precious."*

Chapter Ten

There was silence as we both reflected on his words. Eventually I broke the quiet.

"Some dead were honoured as their bodies passed through Wootton Bassett where the good people of Wiltshire expressed their solidarity, and showed compassion to the grieving relatives. There were no parades for me and the many who lived. I did not expect or want my return to be celebrated, what I did not anticipate was that I would be ostracised by people I had known all of my life. Of course, I realised that kids would mock me, but there is a vast difference between the appreciation that something may take place, and it actually happening.

"Oi cripple" the flocks of crow like kids on bikes would shout as my stick and I tip tapped along the pavement towards the Coop, returning minutes later with a precarious pint of milk and a newspaper. "Long John Silver" they would taunt me passing ever closer, almost touching, but not quite. Someone must have told them about that character, I don't think any of them had read "Treasure Island" or indeed much at all. Perhaps, they knew that I was en ex-soldier – after all, it was a small place and words soon spread - and back in the day they would not have ventured close. But now, I was bent out of shape. They passed closer trying to rile me, the scent of Lynx and laughing gas (their drug of choice) mixing with that of the rancid adolescent male. But they did not or could not; their touch and their taunts were nothing. Death had already placed his hand on me.

Although I knew I was not alone, I suppose I had expected more, but, it had always been this way. Soldiers are magnificent when they are complete yet mostly forgotten when they are not. It wasn't only the mockery of the kids - I had been a pillock like them once myself. It was the lack of gratitude. I was disfigured, rejected, unemployed and perhaps unemployable. My phantom lost limbs still ached. When no one looked I trembled and twitched. I and others like me were wrongs that were hushed up.

I guess that I expected more in the Club, a once widespread institution with one in every village, a place where working men could seek refuge from wives and work. This one, although bucking the trend and remaining open, had seen better days; it was dog-eared and decaying with few forthcoming attractions on a notice board which would once have trumpeted bands, comedians (including some very well-known ones) and bingo, but it now kazoo-ed only an Open Mic (where performers played for free) and televised football. The regulars still nursed their pints like treasure, and - in common with barflies everywhere - had the same conversation every evening.

On my first night back there were shouts of "Welcome home Lad" and "Good to see you" alongside the more mumbled "Sorry to hear about…" which would be accompanied by gazes drifting towards my former leg and my plastic hand. There were pints lined up on the bar, and my back was repeatedly slapped. We had all been changed by the intervening years. My own eyes were now shaded, half closed. At first, I thought this was because of the desert, the extreme intense sun which a lad from cloudy Durham would never get used to. But upon my return my eyes did not widen, they remained the scrutinising, careful, assessing, deliberating eyes of a soldier which made people feel even more uncomfortable. Another barrier had been erected.

We lived in a place which had nothing much to distinguish it. The only building over two storeys is what used to be The Salutation pub; it is now a convenience store, a change which wasn't that convenient for those who liked a decent pint. The buildings squat on the landscape - houses merging with one another, front lawns drifting into open greenspace. Dwellings distinctly northern in appearance and outlook. In the south all plots would have been carefully segregated with picket fences, walls, or hostile hedges but not here. Structures were short so as perhaps not to draw attention to themselves, or because they wished to avoid the view. In the distance was what was once the largest private housing estate in Europe. Known locally as "Valium Valley" it housed hundreds of aspirant couples and their broods. Held together by an antipathy towards their council house neighbours, the aforementioned medication, and a tendency to express their identity through the inconsequential. Kitchens, cars, schools, and holidays are the battlegrounds, each couple searching to assert their superiority. It was a place which did not know the meaning of "enough."

I knew the streets well enough through long lost friends, many of whom I first met at the local community centre which had been home back in the day to a Saturday night heavy rock disco.

Valerie and I had many conversations about where we should set up home. We came very close to buying a house in the "Valley" but knowing we would not fit in we eventually settled on a characterful place a few miles up the road. After thirty years of an old couple's gentle neglect, everything in it creaked, dripped, or rattled. I appreciate I am not sounding too much like an estate agent here, but it was to be our project, and over time we would fix what was damaged or dangerous, and change what we did not like. Valerie would manage everything, and I would do the manual, lumpen stuff when I returned on leave. We had already made good progress, but there was still more to be done.

Following my return from the rehabilitation unit Valerie was wonderful. Her Dad had been injured in a mining accident some years before, so she was used to shattered men. In the long-established tradition of forthright Northern women, she juggled our new-born, silk skinned baby and her two-limbed husband. She organised, she fed, nurtured, hugged. She arranged for old friends and neighbours to call around, to keep my mind occupied and my spirits up.

Over cups of tea, sometimes something stronger, we would tiptoe around each other.

"So, what exactly did you do out there?" was a common question. How do you reply?

"We were fighting for peace. Trying to build something better.

Give the people there a chance, give the girls an education, you know…"

But what I really felt, what the voice inside me was saying was more brutal and more honest.

"Oh, I killed fifty-three people, thirty-eight at distance. I saw twelve of our lads killed and quite a few more badly injured. And, if I am honest, I do not think what we did made the slightest difference. And every night, as I try to sleep, I see faces contorted in pain, eyes closing for the last time and the dark cloak of Death gathering…"

Of course, I never said what I felt; our conversations were good natured, but tame, increasingly dominated by baby Angela.

Sleep is perhaps the drug that in this world of ours is in the shortest supply; ask any parents of new-born children. Of course, I took my turns feeding our voracious little girl while her mother slept. This time when all of the rest of the world seemed to be asleep was so special. Once her milk had been guzzled she would, led by her beautiful button nose, snuggle into me. Twenty two pounds of baby pinning fourteen stones of Dad to an armchair.

It was early November, and I had been home for just under a year. It was early evening and we were sitting quietly watching some candy-floss television. Curtains were open, so we could see the night sky. There was a sudden flash, crash and then a shower of sparks. In an instant I grabbed Valerie, who was nursing Angela, and threw us all to the floor with a scream of

"DOWN!" That was the first time I saw my wife truly cry; she was to spend her life with a man fractured in mind and body, who would forever be frightened of fireworks.

Angela was eighteen months old when the nightmares came for the first time. Although I don't think that I had done it consciously, the excitement, euphoria, and fear of being a parent had left no room for the memories which had been shunted to my mental attic, and the door locked. It was eleven o'clock or so, and Valerie had gone to bed, exhausted, and if not happy, content. I turned off the TV and put on the radio, looking for something gentle to sooth our daughter who was showing no signs of snooze. I eventually settled for a talk show on a local station. The first few calls were innocuous enough someone publicising a local food festival, talking about the celebrity chefs who were coming and the range of produce on offer. There was a woman who had cycled around Britain. It was all positive affirming stuff. And then, even before he had uttered a complete sentence, I knew the next caller's story by his tone, the way the words fell, and the deep gaps between them. He was a veteran who had served, was damaged and had returned to an empty life. I know that I should have turned it off, or tuned to another station, but I couldn't.

The caller spoke of a tree, the Survivor Tree in New York City, the solitary one which remained following the destruction of 9/11. He said it had become a symbol of strength and was now a beacon of green-leafed light. The presenter, who had not heard the story before thanked him. "There are times" the caller said "when I feel just like that tree. Alone. Covered in the dust of death, carrying the weight of those I knew who deserved to live more than I. All light is blood-streaked darkness. Survivors are crushed by their guilt." The six second delay which all live broadcasts use to stop the worst words, did not filter this man's sorrow.

Within five minutes I was sobbing, my tears cascading over my daughter's head.

If you are an injured serviceman and discharged because of your injuries, once you navigate the labyrinth of forms you receive a lump sum compensation payment from the government. Someone somewhere is able to put a price on each lost limb. The money, which if I'm honest was to us a small fortune, means you do not have to work for a while, but that perhaps in a perverse way casts a shadow which makes everything darker.

Although our bank balance was healthy, I needed the validation which comes from work. So, my days were a blur of job hunting, household chores, feeding, walks and baby play, against the backdrop of the increased presence of Valerie's parents. Her Mum had recently retired, her father having done so on medical grounds sixteen years before. With nothing to keep them in Ashington, they sold up, and moved nearby.

Although I accept - as a father with a daughter - that no one will ever be good enough for her, Valerie's parents expected me to be a cross between Prince Charming and the Dalai Lama. I disappointed them. Still, the days I could mostly endure. The nights? No.

Nightmare is too weak a word to describe what haunted my sleep. I always thought that we - my comrades and I - were on the side of the angels; but I learned some time ago that not all angels are a force for good. Not all wrap their wings around you and lift you up; some suffocate and drag you down, there are still fallen and falling angels. My night-time mind became a hideout for these devils which spoke in my own voice reminding me ceaselessly and unremittingly of the most horrific things I had ever seen. A slow-motion, voiced over terror, with all of the characters on the wide screen of my mind well known to me, the soundtrack a chorus of screams from the very marrow of their bones. Lost friends and comrades were taunting me for having survived where they did not, "Why was I so special?" was their refrain. I had counted myself lucky. I *now* reckoned myself guilty. I was not special; they should have lived and not I. Their derisory words, fell like drops of ink into the water glass of my mind. Everything became clouded. I replayed every incident, every mission, every patrol, critically reviewing each and every one for what more I could have done. An earlier word of warning, a hastier response, a more accurate shot, a quicker run, or a dressing applied with more pressure and precision. The dead began to assemble in my dreams, a congregation of the killed. Their message, that I had betrayed them, and did not deserve to live.

I soon began to fear what had once been my friend and my solace; sleep.

Increasingly, as the days drifted by all I wanted to do was to hide away, turn out the light, wrap my arms around my head, roll into a ball and be forgotten. I tried to reach out to my now distant brother and sisters, but calls and texts were not returned. They were still angry I had not been there when Mam and Dad were laid to rest. I could not talk to anyone, who else could understand, and even if they did would they judge me and find me guilty? Would they hold me in even less regard than they did now? Because of my service, for some I was still a hero, of sorts, although one from an unpopular or at best misunderstood war which in many minds was combined with the one in Iraq.

I can remember vividly the millions of normal people who in February 2003, marched with their "Stop the War" banners, and how a previously popular, and in touch, Labour Prime Minister had allied himself with a right-wing US President to fight the latter's crusade. Tony Blair proclaiming that "Now was not the time to err on the side of caution." Maybe the river of marchers, including all of those respectable housewives from suburbia who had never done that sort of thing before, had been proved right; in both wars – Afghan and Iraq - there was no great victory, just a fickle, fluid front line which moved, but only for a short while. One moustachioed or bearded villain replaced by one or more others.

The allies themselves did not know what they sought to achieve, let alone how to really defeat their enemy. Shock and awe soon faded. Afghan needed to be put back together, but as so-called liberators we seemed to be better at breaking than building. There was, as there always is, money for bombs but not enough for bricks. We did not establish a credible police force, so there was no sustainable security. Yes, we would swoop into the borderlands and arrest or shoot Taliban and al-Qaeda fighters, but we would not stay long and each spring a new bloom of zealots would gather, budded in the Pakistan winter, blown westward by warmer weather. We did not provide secure jobs. There was a vacuum waiting to be filled. As Mullah Omar once said, "The Americans may have the clocks, but we have the time."

The war resulted in hundreds of thousands of lives torn apart, countless Afghan casualties and the five thousand counted coalition dead. We came to bring the people a better life, and free them from oppression. We expected to be treated like the liberators of Paris in 1944; with the fighting over, democracy would like a benevolent banner unfurl and fix this ancient country. But the all-powerful allies were unable to hold back the very air of this place which has always, since the time of Alexander the Great, blown back invaders, and demolished whatever they had built, or re-built what they had torn down. Unsurprisingly we failed to defeat the enemy and we left a country and a region in turmoil.

My beloved Valerie had her own struggles, she needed to go back to work, not only because of her failure of a husband and his inability to provide a regular income for his family, but also for her own wellbeing. She needed to feel she was something more than a mother, and carer. My in-laws; Valerie's mother the shape and sound of a broken bell, and her father who always looked at me from the corner of his eyes, with scarcely disguised contempt, they both held me responsible for their daughter's unhappiness. They were right.

My father-in-law had never recovered from his own injury. He cursed it, himself, and increasingly others. As his body weakened his cursing grew stronger. He had once been good with his hands, but he was now unable to tie his own shoelaces, the furniture, bird-boxes, and wooden toys he once took pride in, he no longer made. I should perhaps have learned from his experience, saw his path, and avoided it, but self-pity is a well paved road.

You feel lost, so you do what many have done before you, you drink. One day after another in the Club where hours crawl by. Time you should be elsewhere, time you should be with your lovely wife and beautiful daughter, time you should be celebrating what is, instead of mourning what is lost. You occasionally shake yourself out the rut. I had several jobs which friends or family arranged for me, I lasted longest re-stocking shelves in a supermarket, the routine, the straightforwardness of it appealed to me, at least at first. My prosthetic arm ached, and my leg stump burned, but at least I was doing something useful. The fluorescent lights, the piped music, the rainbow of tins and packets stacked floor to ceiling, the throng of shoppers, another less deadly uniform and the comradeship of sorts. It all helped to keep the shadows away for a while, until the time when a customer who could have been Phil's twin walks by the deli counter. Minutes later your colleagues find you huddled in a backroom, in a ball, weeping and wailing. After that I could not go back.

You stop looking in the mirror, the man you once thought vaguely handsome, the one who "scrubbed up well" has become a shadow of his former self. Valerie would still hug and smile but with every day those smiles became emptier, there were more words she couldn't speak, more mascara tears wiped away before she hoped I would see them, but the small dark smudges always remained.

Some of the street corner beggars I knew before I joined up were ex-soldiers, and perhaps that should have been a warning. Ostracised and disfigured, faces old before their time, they sat limbless, hopeless or both, trembling, and twitching their caps pushed forward to catch coppers. It is only now I think of the wrongs that made these men, the wrongs that were and are hushed up.

People try to help but sometimes the words they use, their helpful observations, become twisted by your own mind. Each comment is heard as negative, and taken to heart. Soon I felt that everything I did was wrong. Each voice added to the chorus of criticism, a Gregorian chant which pointed out every one of my many, many mistakes, and failings.

Perhaps, I should have sought out someone to talk to about my experiences, of years trying to bring peace to a land where everything changes with the dawn. Perhaps I ought to have found someone to talk to about the battles and fights, the heroism, brutality and cowardice. Perhaps I should have found someone to talk to about the life-changing / life-ending bomb. Perhaps I ought to have found someone to talk to about the loss I felt for my dead comrades. Perhaps I should have done many things, but I felt I could not, I felt trapped, and the more time passed, the more imprisoned I became.

But you carry on, every day you try again, you know that you will probably fail, but in the words of Samuel Beckett you try to fail better. On one particular day my challenge, my opportunity was to decorate a bedroom. Ah Jack, as you yourself know, it is not always as easy as it appears. I was up a ladder paint pot in hand, brush dipping in and out like a hummingbird, the wall changing, coming alive with new colour. My muscles were aching and tingling from concentration, I went to step down but could not and did not. It shouldn't have but the knee of my prosthetic leg locked, my leg went between the rungs, I fell face first, my nose flattening against the floorboards, paint splattering around and on me.

I howled, my face crumpled, not because of the pain, but because of my own inadequacy. I had once been a warrior, a master of my destiny, I was now nothing more than a broken civilian, raging, doubtful and terrified of failure.

I had failed again but I had failed worse. Black dogs, the first one which had been by my side for years had enlisted his friends, they now howled and snarled around me. I was overcome. You leave because you are fearful of what you may become, you are afraid of what terror you may inflict upon your girls. You come from a family of sometimes angry men, and the life of every man is touched by intimations of his father, in my case, an anger which can become a roaring lion seeking something to devour.

That day, that moment, I felt it was better to go than to stay. Durham is a place which is easy to leave. I left as many before me have done on a National Express bus, the 13:00 to London Victoria. At the bus station with 15 minutes to spare, I rummaged through the bookshelves of a nearby charity shop. For a pound Dante's "Divine Comedy" became my companion, at least for a while. Early on, in the first few pages its narrator loses his way in a dark wood "in the middle of the journey of life."

Jack smiled ruefully, *"I remember that poem, beaten into us it was "How savage wild that forest, how robust and rough it grows." I didn't appreciate its value, or its truth at the time."*

A wistful pause, I carried on. "As the bus pulled away in its haze of blue-grey smoke, the reflection in the window glass asked me what circle of hell was assigned to those who would never again see their wife and child.

I know something about hiding in a barren landscape, but you know the easiest place to hide is in the company of others, among millions of strangers. All Underground stations have a repeated announcement of "Mind the gap" which is delivered in the tones of a robotic headmaster. But it is not, necessarily, the gap between platform and train that should most worry you. London is a city of gaps. The streets are not, as you said earlier Jack paved with gold, in some ways they are not paved at all. Drawn by hope of rebirth or redemption, many tens of thousands migrate to the city every year. Some find a place – at least for a while. Countless others wander but become lost. The stern-faced, closed-down shutters of an austerity ravaged state treat you as unworthy, the undeserving homeless. You ask for help to tide you over until you can get a job, they tell you to wait six weeks as though you too need to suffer forty days and nights in the wilderness. Some of the richer councils pride themselves on having the lowest property taxes in the country, those who can afford multi-million-pound homes are not asked to pay their fair share, it is a world turned upside down, those in need have little to help them.

You resort to begging, and at this time - only this time - you are glad, although you curse your sorry self for this thought, that your parents are dead so they cannot see you like this. They can't see you scrapping and scratching, trying to scrape together the twenty-three pounds that will give you an occasional night in a hostel where a clean bed and a hot shower restore, and make you human for a while. When you're not there, and those hostel nights are few and far between, you hide, in subways, car parks, by restaurant bins, or if you're lucky in the parks which they lock at night to keep the nocturnal, human animals out.

There is a poster in London which is designed to discourage the theft of scooters and bikes. The line is "the more secure your bike is, the less visible it is to thieves." Well, I now think with people the reverse is probably true, the less secure you are, if you are unable to engage, express, or spend you are pushed to the fringes of people's vision, you become unseen. In the eyes of most people you blend into the landscape, four feet below them, the kindly toss you a quid, others stare like Medusa, turning you to stone.

So, you seek out your kind: ancient stones. In cathedrals and churches you are able to lose yourself amongst those that kneel in prayer before their immortal incompetent God. If my presence in these dark, quiet places could be construed as a sign of some deep-seated belief in him, she, or it; there was never a sign that those feelings were reciprocated.

Days seem like weeks, and weeks seem like an eternity. Everything begins to ache, you become a feast for the tiny creatures, an axis of weevils, who have always been there but have been suppressed by a clean body, fresh clothes, and an unpolluted mind. All that you used to take for granted - to eat, to sleep, to wash - is trouble and pain. There seems to be no glimmer of blue, the sky is always dark, forbidding and foreboding. And when the sun goes down, shadows grow longer and the human beasts appear.

You are afraid and ashamed. Every thought is a circle of regret. You begin to look at your heart and everything you have ever done, and it all looks black. You become blinded by what you see as the brilliance and light of others, you feel less and less in a city that screams for more. In yourself you see only emptiness in your once bright eyes. All around you is striving, purposeful, and even the buildings grasp and grow higher. You are reminded of your old grammar school motto, we had one too Jack." A shared smile. "Ours was "Nintendo Surgimus," to strive, to rise. You do neither. You do not want to touch, feel, see, hear, or taste. You have no sense, so you yearn for no feeling. Afraid and ashamed, you lay down your weary head, all you want to do is to sleep, but even the night, the once welcoming darkness turns its back on you. Your nightmares also caught the bus, all of your dreams have grown teeth.

My penance for once having held the power of death over others was to roam this land wraith-like. In roaming I soon began to fade."

A white police van drew up to the kerb where its two officers alighted. A moment later two torches beamed at me. Stern faced, the officers did not. "Are you okay?" asked the taller of the two. I nodded. A wave of acknowledgement. They got back in their vehicle and drove off.

"I am not the only one to care about you." Once again, Jack tried to lift my spirits.

Chapter Eleven

I needed to continue with my story as I felt that Jack did not yet understand me.

"Days blur with the same struggle, you lose track of dates until your discarded newspaper duvet pulls you up short, reminding you of red letter days – birthdays and anniversaries which you no longer celebrate. I became, and remain a shrunken, sunken, shadow of a man, all I want to do is pass to the shadow world yet you, a shadow yourself refuse me my final choice. What right have you?!" The last short sentence snarled.

"London is a city stuffed with art galleries, the type of places I would frequent in my youth, where gilt frames imprison beauty, joy, love, loss, myth, man, suffering and pain. Although I would gaze at those old oil paintings with their tiny cracks I did not see what the 'old masters' were telling me, but, I had little knowledge of life then. I always felt the painter had imprisoned the subject and emotion, but they could not be caged forever. Perhaps, they would remain paint jailed for a few centuries, before escaping, emerging through one wispy, hairline crack at a time. Eventually, another picture would emerge, perhaps the one the artist most wanted to reveal. Perhaps this imprisoned art is a premonition for life itself. I know that each new wrinkle, line, and crack on my own face enable my own heart-felt emotions to seep through.

My mind became a cacophony, I retreated from London in search of silence. I needed hills, remote valleys, ragged coastlines – people-less places where ravens cawed, woodpeckers drummed, owls warned of the coming night and gulls serenaded the waves. I had often sought out wilderness in my youth, content to be on my own, the wildness of nature soothing my restless spirit.

That was some weeks ago, although the sound of traffic and the noise of others disappeared, the chatter within my head did not. There was no longer anything to drown out my own clamour. Whenever I tried to forget or to forgive, my mind catapulted me back, snagged as I have always seemed to be, since that fateful day, on the barbed wires of memory.

It was one of the long, dark nights when you stare out across the sand-strewn, fly-blown desert. Phil and I were on watch, there were hours to run, we were talking - quietly, cautiously - to keep ourselves awake. He was telling me about a quieter place which he had been to some years before. It was supposedly the quietest place on earth. In Minnesota, at the Orfield Laboratories, there is an anechoic chamber. It is so silent that you become the noise, at first your beating heart, and the fan like swish of eardrums, then the sounds that go on without you noticing. The clank of each organ pulsing, the hum of life within. The sound of each individual hair growing, and the low-level scream of millions upon millions of dying cells. Phil went there feeling that he would lose himself, and be nurtured in the chamber's womb. He lasted thirty-five minutes before, overcome, and unable to orientate himself, he fell to the floor, then crawled, baby-like to the door. "It is" he said, when some months later he told me of the event "only when you experience total silence that you become aware of its peril."

Two years or so later, there I was imperilled. On a hill somewhere in the South Downs where the relative silence outside, seemed to add to the noise within me.

Your never restful mind flits, a hedge full of Old Man's Beard with its long delicate threads, brings you back to what your grandmother once told you about Armistice silk. Material that had been used in the Great War for munition bags, was sold at the end of the conflict at a knock-down price to the textile trade where it was treated and turned into civilian garments. I feel that all of us ex-soldiers are a lot like Armistice silk, we try to be re-purposed, but we cannot escape the smell of gunpowder.

Your churning mind sifts like an archaeologist through layers of emotion and memory. Alone, you think of love, the unceasing, unchallenging, forever-accepting fire of devotion, passion so strong it may be raised by a breath or a word, attachment which is nurtured by each caress.

Alone you doubt. Have I ever known all of the aspects of love? Have I ever felt its embrace? Has my spine ever tingled at the thought of another? Has my heart ever leapt with joy or trembled sparrow like within my breast?

Oh yes. Once there was love, I see it now, it is far, distant. Valerie and I had love, that real love which shines like a fleeting shaft of sunlight on a shore, but it became drowned out by the clatter of my failure, and the quiet cry of absence of those parts which were lost forever.

Whatever love there is for me I do not deserve it. I am not, and probably never was worthy. Now I fear this life more than I have ever feared death. Death to me is commonplace, life something to be freely taken. My fifty-fourth kill will be myself. I am nothing, I will be dust, and no one will know or care. Unidentified, there will be a single mourner at my pauper's 9 a.m. funeral, and he shall be the Council Officer there not for love, but duty. My unremarkable short life will be forgotten as the last sod is placed over my cheap coffin.

I am not the man Valerie married, I am not the dad baby Angela deserves. The world will not skip a beat when I go. My voice had gone from a scream to a whisper, and my touch now had no more substance than the ghost of a spider's web. I had become Aeolian, the only sound I now make is when the wind whistles through me, but now, the sky and the sea have settled, everything is still, even the air has deserted me…"

Chapter Twelve

"*B*ut *I have not*" Jack looked at me.

"*What have I learned in my short life and my much longer death? I think I have discovered that we are all treasured, there are those who love us accepting our imperfections - the real and*" he paused "*the imagined. Friend, know that tomorrows are never perfect, today is all we will ever have. Hold it before it goes.*"

Waves, and their pull on the pebbled beach filled the silence.

Jack, who now seemed lost in his own thoughts, did not yet wish to return to his own tale. The silence became heavy, I filled it.

"On the streets every penny has to count double and you can no longer afford to buy books; even second-hand charity shop ones are beyond your reach. So you hang on to what you have, you inhale every sentence. Words become a safety net which is always there, and although the pages become musty, tear and rain wrinkled, the text is always fresh. Alongside Dante, one book, a collection of comic verse, was always in my pocket. The poems of Edward Lear, Ogden Nash, Roger McGough and the prolific ANON helped to remind me that somewhere, even if it became increasingly hard to find, I still had a smile.

When you can, you spend time in libraries. The rules are usually that provided you do not cause a fuss, and you do not drink or eat you can stay as long as you want. But libraries are now harder to find, they are either closed, or dependant on volunteers and open for just a few hours a day. When you are able to find one your heart leaps, not just because of the shelter, safety, and warmth but because of the expanse of unread pages and as yet unknown stories.

You are mostly alone but there are times, particularly on market days when libraries tend to fill, and then you become aware that you are one of the great unwashed. The polite people try to mask it, the fact that you have invaded their space and nostrils. The less considerate bark and growl. Books however always embrace you."

I had become tired of my own voice, and the feelings it stirred. It was time for my tongue to rest.

"I have been rambling on." I said "My apologies. Please tell me more of your own story."

Jack's eyes left the reflections on the now still sea.

"Very well. By the winter of 1773 my money was all spent. Many of my companions and associates had either been apprehended by the Runners, or had disappeared. I felt that I had to leave London. I vowed to discover for myself whether the New World was indeed the vision on the hill, but, unable to borrow, and now because of the tightening net, unwilling to steal I could not pay my own passage to the American Colonies. My only option was to travel as an indentured servant who, if I survived the typhus, dysentery, fever, and other travails of the voyage, would be sold. I would then work for my new master for between four and five years without

pay but with food and lodging. Still, life as a servant was - at least I though at the time - far better than a long spell in a London gaol or, my most likely fate, a short spell on the gallows.

There were times at sea I would have willingly thrown myself into the foam. It appeared I was not the first to consider death a better option than bondage; there were nets (capacious, secured, thick roped) around the ship to catch those who attempted to take their own lives. After all, a drowned passenger was a loss to the shipowner of between fifteen and twenty pounds. Within the ship we were stacked and arranged for efficiency and profit with barely a hand-width between me and my neighbour. Many of my fellow passengers did not reach the New World. Typhus ran through the ship like a hunted fox. Beyond brackish water there was no treatment or relief from the attendant pain and fever.

No night's sleep was ever unbroken, below deck in the stench, fumes, and horror we were all surrounded by screaming, pain-wracked near ghosts.

Those in the last phase of life were hauled to the gunwales. Some took days to die, their screams - as muscle spasms and cramps crushed their drenched yet desiccated bodies - haunt me still. The musket-ball grey sea was infinite, some of the older sailors told tales of the mighty Kraken rising from the depths. Indeed, if you have a mind to imagine such, the white crest of each wave could very easily be the saliva of the vast creature, its appetite whetted by the bones and blood of those who were about to sink beneath the swell."

Once again, Jack gazed out across the Solent at the wisps of sea foam.

Chapter Thirteen

Another pause, this one longer than the last, as the ghost went back into the depths of his memory. He continued.

"After what seemed like an eternity, some of us arrived in the sweet-smelling city of Jamestown, Virginia; which first saw me thin as a famished rat, covered in lice, dressed in rags and with a beard like sea blown foam. On the following day, newly washed and shorn, dressed, and made to appear respectable, we were led to the slave market. Placards were placed around our necks indicating our skills and attributes. Mine read something like: grammar school educated and quick-witted. We were then inspected by our potential owners, a process more worthy of the purchase of a horse. Ears and teeth were checked, breathing was listened to and fingers and toes were counted. Following this, I was exhorted to read. I plucked up my courage knowing that if I adequately demonstrated this skill, I would be of greater value to a potential master and be spared some of the more menial tasks. I was sold for twenty-four pounds - a labourer's wages for a year - to a Mr. Graham a gentleman who owned a large tobacco plantation. Although in the future I may indeed be given some clerical tasks, my master wished for me to understand how his business operated. So I, a free-born Scotsman was set to work in the fields alongside slaves; how my world had fallen in. The work was unremitting, the overseers brutal, and the food meagre. Nothing had prepared me for this living hell. The sun which I had previously looked upon as a rarely seen and benevolent spirit, broiled and baked me. Day

after day of incessant heat. I was blinded by sweat as I swatted at insects of every colour and shape, missing most, those who avoided my flailing hands bit without mercy. My white skin which soon became a vivid patchy crimson, at least saved me from the brutal floggings that my fellow black slaves suffered. Within days their shoulders, backs and legs were scarred. My own hands became so blistered, scratched and cut that every grip or action was an act of pain.

Whenever I rested or sought to ease my battered body the overseer thrashed me with verbal barbs. My fellows, even though our languages were alien, offered me their words of solace and, I believe. their prayers. Even though it had been some years since I last entered a church, I found myself forming words learned long ago. One particular phrase filled my mind and my mouth as I gazed upon the easy brutality of the overseers, "in as much as you have done it unto one of my brethren ye have done it unto me." The bloodiness of the plantation confirmed one long abiding thought, under the skin all men are the same. Days and weeks passed. My spirit was ebbing, like a flame guttering and coughing in a gale. If I stayed, I was sure that I would soon die. Among the slaves, all of whom came from the west coast of Africa, kingdoms whose names I did not recognise at the time and have now forgotten, there was a sinewy, ramrod-straight man who was knotted like a walking cane. He prayed, both in the Christian services which the Master insisted we all attend, and whilst working in the field to whatever god he had carried in his heart across the water. He prayed to numb the monotony and pain, and to be free. He prayed for his family, thousands of miles away. He prayed for his fellow slaves.

He also prayed for me who he called "The Red Man." Indeed, the colour of my hair and skin had become one and the same.

Over time we learned to communicate, we told each other of the lives we had lived, and our wishes for the future.

The black slaves would sing to remind themselves of home, they would sing as they worked the fields – the music a balm to soften the pain, they would sing to praise their gods. They would sing unceasingly. Perhaps the most poignant song was the one which I learned translated as "My Master bought me, so he will not kill me."

These stoic songs fanned my own dimming flame. Hopefully my destiny was not to die in some rancid field, my brief time as a highwayman had convinced me that even I - with all of my faults and weaknesses – could, perhaps achieve something of note. In order to do that I needed to escape.

After some weeks - my back breaking baptism now over - I was entrusted with recording details of the crops sown in a series of fields, of producing bills of lading, and writing business letters on behalf of Mr. Graham. There was much work to be done, and although it was undoubtedly far more comfortable than the field, the working day ran, candle-lit, well into the evening. Many years since school, it had been some time since I had had to concentrate so hard, my head ached, my hand cramped, my fingers blackened with ink. Aye, it was hard at first but I soon grew more and more capable. It was the second or third week of my time in the plantation office when I chanced upon the records kept by Mr. Graham of all the slaves and servants in his employ or ownership. Of course I read my own first: average height and build, red hair, green eyes, hands both paint dyed, a slight stammer, nothing much to mark him out. In a way I was disappointed at my relative anonymity, but it together with the swift horses of paper, pen, and ink which lay in front of me were the means of my escape.

When travelling, from place to place all servants needed a pass signed by their master explaining their movements. By looking out for one another and challenging any stranger who crossed their path, plantation owners attempted to deter escapees. It was my conviction that with a convincing counterfeit pass, my quick mind, and sufficient supplies which could be collected gradually over many weeks, I would be able to reach a town far enough away from Mr. Graham's plantation to be safe, and free. I made the necessary preparations to take my leave. Just after midnight with August's full moon at my back I headed north.

For perhaps the first time in my life I was alone for hours and days on end. Of course in London as a highwayman I had robbed alone, but soon afterwards I would find myself in the warm embrace of a tavern and the yet-warmer embrace of a woman. But here, there was no one for mile upon mile, in comparison the Great North Road thronged with humanity. Forever used to cities and the cheek by jowl human cacophony of desire, deceit, death, and drunkenness, I very soon discovered that I was afraid of the true wild. In the plantation fields there had been tales of bears, wild boars, wolves, and snakes - many, many snakes. Around me was the overwhelming ripeness and abundance of summer, there were snuffles, grunts, howls and cries, bird calls which were more banshee than blackbird. My eyes were alert and wide, my heart beat an un-remitting tattoo. Perhaps I had read too much Ovid as stories of mythical beasts and trickster gods flickered across my mind. For many days and nights I barely slept thinking that every noise heralded my doom. It was only on the fifth night as I sat beneath a shimmering stand of birch trees that sleep finally overtook me. I collapsed with exhaustion; my dreams, once a place where I was always strong, were now full of shadowy terrors. I awoke in the cold dew of the next day surprisingly alive albeit covered with hungry, persistent ants.

Increasingly my days and nights became less fraught. Although I feared being hunted by the packs of wolves which I heard howling in the distance, I only ever saw one. It was an underwhelming beast, although I now know that when you see one many more are gazing at you. The great creatures of the continent, which filled the fireside tales of my own and other plantations, were thankfully, mostly, elsewhere, apart from one memorable occasion which I will you about in a moment. With the distance between me and my owner increasing by the day I grew more confident, moving from forest trails and clawing undergrowth to the roads, which though muddied and rutted were easier and quicker to navigate.

On the roadside grew profusions of berries, a mixture of deep red, blue, and black. I had tasted some on the plantation from where the fields shook hands with the forest, guided in my tasting by those who knew this land, its bounty, and its dangers. On my journey north I was sustained by these sweet capsules of goodwill which were sprinkled freely by an unseen hand for me, and the wasps, my *striped ever-present companions. One evening in what I believe was late August, (although I attempted to track the days their route was soon lost to me), I spied a particular luscious bush, heavy with fruit, its boughs almost breaking, berries brushing the floor. The day had been hard, there had been no isolated farms from which to purloin bread or any human food, and I was ravenous, my stomach churning and twisting as though preparing to eat itself. Frenzied, I ran headlong into the bush, forcing handfuls of berries into my open mouth, as I chewed juice ran like a mountain stream through my stubble and onto my shirt. I must have been in my heady state for ten minutes or more before there was a rustle as a branch fluttered, then shuddered, and shook. There was a low bull-like groan, two bass notes, followed by two more before they merged into a sound which was as though the earth itself was snoring deep in wine filled sleep. The branch nearest me which not so long ago brushed the ground moved to one side. Two enormous berries, strangely round and brown with no blush of grey or hint of sweetness sat with no support from branch or stem. A short snout pushed forward, its moist nose snuffling and inhaling me. Five claws emerged, long, sharp, and deadly. Another pawful emerged from my right.*

Right in front of me gazing thoughtfully as though at its next meal was a black bear, large, beautiful, and dangerous. I had seen the brown cousins of these magnificent creatures before, manacled on street corners, dancing to the wheezy tune of an accordion and the ping of coins being thrown into a hat. This free-born bear was not cowed, it controlled its own destiny, and my own future.

At times like this you re-discover prayer, the dusty practice that you neglect for so long. I prayed ferociously, rapidly, and fervently to be left alone, I wished no harm on the creature, but the priority of course was that no harm should befall me. There was no immediate response, didn't God appreciate that this was an urgent matter? In that particular moment I was prepared for death, ready for my life to be torn from me, my hot blood to cover the leaves, and my flesh to be food for the beasts of the field, primarily the one directly in front of me.

The bear seemed curious at my lack of panic, and perhaps it was a change in the light as a cloud passed over the sun, but the dark eyes seemed to soften, the head moved slightly to one side as though the creature were weighing up its options. There was a movement of its jaw, I saw two large yellow teeth, and then two more.

It was then I began to sing, yes, I sang, I do not know what came over me, panic, a surge of alcohol from fermenting berries or perhaps something Holy. I sang, quietly, mouse-like at first, but then rising, lifting, roaring, my eyes tight closed with dreams of light, and glory.

"Breathe on me breath of God,
Fill me with life anew.
That I may love, what thou dost love,
and do what thou wouldst do."

It was a hymn to mark my passing, to accompany my spirit as it rose or fell to its final destination.

There was no pain, and no hurt, had I passed serenely, angel winged to the next life?

The long pink tongue slurped, lolloped, and licked the muzzle, the claws lifted, and then withdrew. I waited for the creature to crash through the undergrowth towards me. Moments passed, the birds which had stilled their song, as they quietly observed the confrontation between man and beast began to once again trill and twitter. The bear was more interested in burying its snout in bushes of berries than in the body of an increasingly thin, sunburned Scotsman.

Perhaps the nymph Callisto herself had returned to earth from the heavens, and spared me. But this was no myth, this bear had granted me a ticket for life, my task? To find a purpose.

I now moved inexorably towards my destination, Philadelphia."

Until that night, those small hours of dark and memory, I have never really, <u>deeply</u> listened to anyone, even Phil or my beloved Valerie. No interruption from me, no desire to demonstrate or share what little knowledge I had. It was a time for me to be and to hear.

Chapter Fourteen

Jack's low, thoughtful voice continued.

"Originally settled by the English then becoming a haven for migrants from Europe, with Swedes, Germans and even Welshmen thronging the streets, and thriving on its trade in sugar, rum and tobacco with the West Indies, Philadelphia was used to the comings and goings of strangers. I reckoned that I would be able to lose myself in the throng. Perhaps I could return to my trade as a house painter. My spirits were high as I entered the bustling city. I marvelled at the well-tended streets, the public gardens, library, hospital, theatre, coffee houses and inns. For the first time in weeks I caught sight of my own reflection with bones too big for my skin, and a red beard which does not suit any man. I soon rented a room, washed, and shaved, and had my shirt laundered. I then slept long, curled in the comfort of a simple bed. The next morning rested and restored I made my way towards the market place, my few coins jangling in my now almost empty purse.

In order to eat and put a roof over my head I needed to find work. Ironically the climate which had so scorched, and almost killed me over the last few weeks was my saviour. The heat and humidity not only cracked my skin it also warped and weathered the windows and doors of each and every home. The dwellings were further beset by the voracious insects of the continent which seemed to resent the very presence of Europeans, as they bit and burrowed in an effort to reclaim each and every of the grand houses, and return them to nature. It was an ideal opportunity for a highly trained painter who had decorated some of the finest homes in London. But I was ill equipped with no name or reputation in this new city, indeed I had no brushes, no tools, and no customers. I needed to make connections.

In this beautiful well-proportioned place, I was once again at some form of peace. No longer a wreck shuddering at the sight of an unknown shadow, or shivering as untamed beasts bellowed beneath the trees. In this spot, nature - at least for the moment - had been tamed: there was a public garden, verdant and glistening; a theatre to restore the soul and lift the spirits, and a library. It was this building which beckoned most to me, hiding in the shadows I had not read for weeks, I was hungry for new words, ideas, and stories. But the books would have to wait for a short while. To exist I needed money, I needed work. The kindly library clerk responded to my enquiries around where someone of my profession may find employment whilst he manoeuvred himself deftly between myself and his beloved books, as if he feared for their safety. He directed me towards a local coffee house where a certain Mister Weatherley could be found.

The London Coffee House stood on the southwest corner of Second and Market Street. I did not enter at first, but stood nearby for some time observing the comings and goings of what looked to be, judging by their briskness, traders, and merchants. Fear of discovery and capture then crossed my mind, perhaps these people may know of or have dealings with my owner Mr. Graham. But even though I was a fugitive and did run the risk of being returned, I needed to work. The three hundred miles between us would surely serve to disguise me, and I had nothing to mark me out (a phrase that would return). Even so my heart raced as my mind went one way and then the other. Finally, after twenty or so minutes, and several walks around the block, I summoned up the courage to push open the doors.

As in every other civilised town or city, coffee houses dominated the commercial and social life of Philadelphia. Having spent many an hour in such places whilst in London I had a sense of what I would encounter. Merchants and ships' captains, travellers, council officials, churchmen, journalists, gentry, and those seeking refreshment gathered in noisy togetherness. There were circles of influence, quiet business discussions in hushed tones with scraping quills, caffeine fuelled bonhomie, the swapping of news and gossip and in one corner a gaggle of disparate, disagreeing voices where opinions were kicked to and fro like fiery, cannonballs. The city had been founded by, and was still dominated by Quakers. Many of the buildings, including the coffee house itself were monochrome reflecting the simple stark dress of the sect. For them colour was an unnecessary addition to the everyday, something to be rationed, fearful perhaps that an excess would cause universal blindness.

I made my way to the counter, and in between the hissings of the copper urn asked the proprietor for a coffee and of the whereabouts of Mister Weatherley.

"Why do you ask sir?" and more pointedly "where are you from?"

I responded courteously.

"Oh" came the icy reply "a Scotsman."

The quiet crept, first there was "hubbub," then "hub," before "h" and then silence.

All eyes were on me and my sunburned yet reddening face.

"A coffee if you please" I repeated my initial request in a whisper. Around me, from the benches and chairs, there was a hiss and a low groan as though a heavy wave was retreating from a shingle beach.

"This place Sir is for gentlemen; your tongue betrays you as not one of that number. Please leave." My nails dug into the flesh of my palms; my lips froze as though in a death mask. Attempting to retreat as elegantly as I could, I raised my lopsided, weather-beaten hat to the proprietor and his customers. "Good day gentlemen" I uttered as loudly and strong as my shuddering self would permit as I strode past the gurning faces towards the door.

Into the dark air I fell, spent, ravaged, and exhausted, I propped myself against a nearby wall. Although London was a hard place with harder people where people of my nationality, and there were many, struggled, I had never felt so utterly and completely alone. I had little money, no contacts, nothing to call upon, nothing to give me substance or succour in this city. Although I had faced despair on many occasions, perhaps this time my nine-lives were reaching an end.

A matter of moments later the door to the coffee shop opened and a man appeared. I began to push myself upright fearing that the quiet violence of indoors would follow me and turn into a beating. "Hold" he called in an English voice. "Do not be afraid, I know of another place that will provide sustenance, even to those of a Scottish persuasion." I regained a glimmer of a smile. He extended his arm and gestured towards a three-story wooden building on a side-street. That was how I first met Thomas Paine.

I subsequently discovered that just a few months before my arrival there had been a mass exodus of Scots from Philadelphia. This was in response to what they felt was the city's increasing radicalisation and disrespect for the Crown which these loyal Caledonians did not wish to be associated with. At first there was distrust and wariness, but with my new friend Thomas as my backer, I soon found work and one well-done job followed another as I rediscovered my metier.

We look into many thousands of eyes as we pass through life; some are blank, some gaze gently at the world, and some, the very few, have eyes like wild tinder boxes. Thomas had such eyes, and fingernails as black as print-soaked pitch.

While I painted with my brush, my new friend Thomas drew with his pen scenes more vivid than I could ever imagine. His life too had been incomplete until he came to America, as dirty and rag wrapped as myself, where with the help of a Scottish bookseller - aye, we folks from Northern Britain have a lot to answer for - he soon discovered his calling. At first he wrote of the everyday using pennames to contribute different perspectives and purported expertise to the Pennsylvania Magazine. Over time his voice developed into one which was plain and straightforward, one which gave life to half formed things, put names to absence, and described the yearning within all of us. In many ways my time in Philadelphia was my schooling. Oh yes at Heriot's, I had painfully learned many things, but here, I learned painlessly more than my mind could contain. Each evening there would be discussions, meetings, and assemblies. The air was thick with new ideas, notions, and visions of an earthly utopia. It was a time for everyman to stir. I read voraciously, many of my books became paint stained as I ran eagerly - and sometimes un-washed - from work to my reading and then on to noisy, energetic debates.

Printing presses clanged and rung as they gave birth to books and pamphlets, whose words almost scorched the page. Thomas, a man who had failed in business, in marriage and as an excise man was now setting the world aflame with his pen. Each one of his tracts had a scent of the new, of spring, of change and yes, each had a tang of brimstone and fire. His words cajoled, challenged, flattered, and held each reader in his grip as though the author were talking to them directly and personally. His words were those of a kindly uncle taking time to answer all of the questions you had long been asking, to tell you of the world as it was before rousing you to take action to make it the better place it could be. He challenged the sacred cows of the world. His favourite word "Why?," his second favourite "We." When not at noisy discussions, my evenings were spent at the printer's shop of Mr. Bell, here I soon became adept at setting, aligning, and inking. What man can resist knowing that he is at the cusp of a great moment, and that he is alongside its greatest architect? In my own small way I felt that I helped to bring Thomas' words to life.

Will, a few minutes ago you suggested that the painter captures a moment but cannot imprison it forever. An interesting notion.

Perhaps we are all canvases upon which each day, each infinitesimal brushstroke, each slight mixing of colour leaves a mark which builds and builds until our own portrait is complete and able to foretell our destiny. Many neglect their own likeness, gazing through and at the gallery of others. My own painting had been a barely legible scrawl on a tenement wall, but in Philadelphia, at Thomas' elbow, my eyes were opened to the cause of the Americans, my gadfly mind hardened into a resolve to serve the cause of liberty as best I could.

My mind and heart were nourished by the writings of my great, if always argumentative friend Thomas.

"The sun never shined on a cause of greater worth. We have it in our power to begin the world again." And with his tongue in his cheek the delightful maxim "there is something very absurd, in supposing a continent to be perpetually governed by an island." For perhaps the first time in my short, unremarkable life I felt alive, inspired by the promise of America. My mind raced, returned to schooldays when the world lay before me as an opportunity, not as a threat. But as years pass the hope of opportunity fades for most. But in that place, then, I felt a purpose and a calling. I felt valued. A phrase Thomas often repeated was one from Plato which reached across the years "The penalty good men pay for not being involved in politics is that they are governed by men who are worse than themselves." We were involved up to our necks.

Of course, there were critics and political enemies who chastised Thomas for his poor education, breeding, and manners. But as he would say in response, "Although we serve an ideal, we cannot always be ideal." And quoting a letter from a London friend of his

"Although improvement makes straight roads, crooked roads with improvement are roads of genius." Thomas, my new Philadelphian friends, and I were all misshapen; perhaps that was the reason we sought to improve this world.

Whilst in Philadelphia, that place of great variety where wooden-shod Dutch mingled with backcountry hunters, grey clad Quakers, and natives from the mountains, I became enlightened. For the first time in my life I had time to think and feel. I left behind my self-inflicted immaturity, as my courage to use my own intelligence grew and my mind filled with possibilities.

My purse became more and more full as the many doors, windows and walls of Philadelphia succumbed to my brush. Strange as it may seem, in the melting pot of the Colonies I was contented for perhaps the first time in my life. But contentment never lasts. One evening Thomas mentioned that a delegation of gentlemen had arrived by ship from Jamestown. There were in Philadelphia to discuss how the political situation was adversely affecting their business. It appeared that one of their number was Mr. Graham. I was perhaps now too well known to hide in-situ for long, in order to preserve my liberty I had to move on, my restless spirit was drawn towards perhaps the most radical of American cities, Boston."

Chapter Fifteen

As a child I had been fascinated by history, whoever would have known that years later I would sit alongside one of its most colourful characters? Jack was now in full flow, long dry memories flooding back to him.

"Boston was rather more welcoming than Philadelphia had initially been. I carried a letter of introduction from Thomas, although in reality it was not needed, as some had heard of my involvement further south, and my reputation - such as it was - had spread. I was soon in work and ingratiated with a band of progressive thinkers which included the radical Sam Adams. There was a growing belief in the colonies that no one in power cared for the hopes or feelings of the citizens there, the King only cared for his tax revenues. My newfound friends came up with an imaginative way to display their dissent, and call out to the tin ear of government...

It was a very cold night but those of us who had gathered on Griffin's Wharf were warm with the flush of liberty. It was not long before sixty or so of us swarmed over the decks of the Eleanor, the Dartmouth, and the Beaver and threw each and every wooden chest of their cargo of East Indian tea, over three hundred of them, into the water. We whooped and we yelled, many of us were dressed as Mohawk Indians, our hair greased, our bodies covered with deerskin shirts and leggings, some with arrow quill and bow. This was partly as disguise, and partly for the child-like joy of dressing up and taking on the appearance and attitudes of another. The message we sent, as the Indian tea darkened the American water, to the distant British government were the four words of our creed "No taxation without representation" a shout which was carried on the western wind all the way to Westminster.

Of course, the British Government did not listen or respond positively to the concerns of the Colonists, they thought they could intimidate and impose their will. The Royal Navy blockaded Boston Harbour so no ships, apart from those of the East India Company - who collected taxes for the far-away government - could bring supplies into the city. The British implemented stronger controls, they drafted in more soldiers, and erected gun-bristled checkpoints on all of the main roads.

When this approach failed, they commenced raids on those towns, villages, and farmsteads they felt were sympathetic to the protest and which they, in their inflammatory terms, referred to as engaging in sedition and treason. They beat, stole, arrested and when there was the inevitable response of resistance, they brutalised. Have you ever seen a farmhouse burn with its inhabitants inside while soldiers take their sport with the daughter who had the misfortune to be caught alone in the barn?"

Once again Jack's long-dead eyes were wide, and the veins throbbed in his neck.

"Have you ever heard the screams of children as the muskets of Hessian mercenaries shoot into their soft, sinless flesh? Have you ever seen pure evil wear a coat of red and carry a flag, ironically consisting of the emblems of saints and martyrs, which purports to be of your own country?

I was lodging in the house of someone whom the British thought sympathetic to the demands of the Colonists. On hearing the approach of soldiers' boots, I hid myself before all others, my cowardice and lack of chivalry driven by my own fear. I crouched, shaking, and sobbing in the shadows as innocents died because their parents or grandparents had the temerity to ask for justice."

"In this febrile time when allegiances and opinions changed with the rising sun there were fewer people who now recognised me as friend. Although George Washington claimed that Thomas' pamphlets were the equal of a regiment in the field, there were some leaders of the revolution who sought to put him and his intemperate words out to grass. There were strong disagreements. Thomas was not one to compromise his ideals, he saw the proposed new republic as an opportunity to rebuild the world anew. Others wanted far fewer changes accusing Thomas and others of displaying a reckless lack of realism. Inevitably those on the side of freedom splintered into sub-groups. Every fracture helped the British whose violent net grew tighter. My close friendship with Thomas was no longer helpful. I was in the midst of a tinderbox which threatened to consume me.

Although America suited my spirit, I now felt an irresistible urge to return home. I was drawn like the salmon. Why? I did not know, but my very blood seemed to thin and tire on foreign soil. There is iron in our blood - as the son of a blacksmith I know this more than most – this element is magnetised by our homeland so we are never able to escape its' draw. We are all eventually pulled towards the Pole Star of home. A combination of fear and blood compelled me to once again cross the great, salt sea.

So, with my remaining money I paid for my passage to Liverpool. Whilst on the way to America the sea had been a constant musket grey, on the return it - like me - had many moods. I was a very different man to the one who had fled England two years before, I was infected with a new spirit - Liberty. As we sailed by Ireland, we were on a shimmering sea, skimmed by shearwaters, the birds taunting the waves with their delicate wing tips. Light dashing through the water as though energised by the nearness of land, like a young lover dizzy with enchantment. Although I arrived in England penniless I knew exactly what to do, I joined the army. You see at the time, even as a private, you received an enlistment bonus of a few shillings. I deserted a whole two days later. The money, kindly given by a garrulous sergeant was just enough to get me started.

I used different names in each of the towns I visited and for each of the two further occasions when I re-joined the army which was always hungry for recruits. As you know the common man fights and bears the brunt of war. I used a rag bag of names - all James: Boswell, Hill and Hinde, the former an author, the second a surgeon and the latter a famous highwayman. These aliases helped me to muddy the trail when I eventually left to pursue other interests.

In order to survive I had to steal food, money, drink – every man needs to celebrate now and again - and anything else that took my fancy. I flapped magpie-like from place to place, although I soon learned that villages are notoriously more difficult for the light-fingered stranger, their residents seeming to have a heightened sense *of danger. No matter, whatever its provenance there was more than enough for me.*

At first you find thievery a strange pastime, indeed it is an unusual profession for a grammar schoolboy and trained artist, but the thing is although at first you find it strange, soon you can't get enough of it. Where tobacco or brandy calms the nerves, filching calms the very fingers themselves - as though they have found their true purpose.

It was asserted by some scribbling journalist writing some years after my death that I had committed a crime in every county of England. Although that may well be the case, I, who have always been circumspect about the veracity of such records, believe that I was blamed for many I did not commit. Then again, I had definitely committed some misdemeanours in both Scotland and Wales which were unreported, so it just goes to show that you cannot trust what you read in newspapers, or indeed some books...

Several of the seven deadly sins, apart from the very deadliest, were my close companions. Avarice always at my shoulder, there were occasional bouts of gluttony when fortune favoured me, and less frequent lustful encounters with those who were charmed by my silver tongue. At first, I wore vice like an ill-fitting garment, but it soon became my skin.

I was once again on my own which I know to be a nightmare for many, but it is a blessing for some. The light, the sounds and the smells of England are so different to those of the Americas. It took me a little while to once again become used to the wails, chitters, growls or snarls of badgers; the piercing screams or the hup, hup,

hup of the fox, or the screech and shriek of the tawny owl. I don't mind telling you there were some jittery, jumpy, and sleepless nights. Soon however you become accustomed. After a while the dark seems to drown out the noise, placing a soft blanket on all who lie beneath it."

I nodded encouraging Jack's words. As we spoke we both began to realise how much we shared.

Chapter Sixteen

Jack's story continued.

"*From then on, nothing truly disturbed my slumber until I made my way through Gloucestershire to Stroud. It was a mill town with wool, water, money, and a feeling that the old pre-Christian religions lie close to the surface. There was a market with easy pickings which helped me on my way. By that point I had taken to sleeping in fields beneath hedges, hidden from roads, after all it was a lawless time and I did not want to be a victim.*

Ale, bread, and cheese inside me I soon wafted to my usual dreamless sleep. Part way through the night, I juddered awake. The moon was full, almost overhead but the light I saw was not mellow and silver but dark, deep, thick, pulsing crimson. I wiped my face hoping that whatever clouded my eyes was temporary but as I looked at my raised hand it too was bloodied. I stood, screamed, and ran this way then the other, but whichever direction I chose I was trapped encased, captured, sheathed in blood and bandages. Exhausted, I threw myself to the floor. I must be in Hell. I screamed and wept until I had no voice and no more tears.

Doctors of the mind say that many of our worst dreams and fears can be explained by the mundane. But my guide to everything, my trusted Ovid, says all dreams are brought to men by the four sons of Somnus the god of sleep. Morpheus and his brothers Icelos, Phobetor and Phantasos who all come on their noiseless wings. Had one of this deceptive brood come to taunt me or show me my destiny? Wrung out and resigned to whatever fate awaited me, I eventually found troubled rest.

The next day came. My first in which circle of hell? I steeled myself for whatever tortures awaited me. But there was no oppressive heat, no demonic cackles, and no scent of sulphur.

In the early light I found myself in a field, stone walls to both left and right, with green, mossy grass beneath my feet. Around me were tens of wooden frames, dripping red with what I thought in that moment were the flailed hides of sinners. I stood slowly, hesitantly not knowing what or who surrounded me. I am still unsure why but I reached out and touched the frame closest to me. I had fully expected a feeling of soft skin, but no, it was softer, delicate, and almost comforting. I was surrounded by a field of frame- hung scarlet cloth. There was a voice from the road, a shepherd calling to his dog as between them they cajoled a flock towards fresh pasture. "Morning sir" I ventured "where am I, and what is this?" I gestured towards the field of red. "Stranger, you are not far from Stroud, and the tenter hung cloth is for our brave soldiers and their redcoats." The shepherd must have sensed my fear. "There is nothing for you to be afraid of." I cried with relief. I then hurriedly left the town and its blood-soaked fields vowing never to return. There are times when in sleep I would find myself in that bloody field, each measure of cloth haunting and taunting me. It is a dream which even brandy could not dispel.

Living in the margins, in the ditches and hedges you become a friend, and respecter of the wild things. You read the land to learn where frost falls and the wind whips. Your map is the night sky -

the ever-present Pole Star, dancing Cassiopeia, proud Orion, and the ever-busy Plough. Ovid tells me in his conspiratorial whisper that the sky is filled with unfortunate mortals and vicious monsters who have been cast into the heavens by jealous, tempestuous gods. Morality tales forever above us in pinpricks of intense light.

As an army deserter, if I had the misfortune to be captured, I would almost certainly die from the thousand lashes I would receive, so I travelled mostly by friendly starlight and hid out, as best I could, by day.

Sometimes however a man on the run needs to feel the refreshing bitter tang of beer on his throat and be surrounded by the presence and chatter of others, even strangers. It was in Oxford, a city filled with educated men of more parts than this fugitive, where stone colleges sprouted, some like All Souls from the slavery of others, that I found refuge and a place to slurp. I was hidden in the shadows of The Eagle and Child Inn. It was far enough away from the places where I had enlisted, so hopefully I could safely slake my thirst without threat. From my quiet corner I overheard a group of tradesmen discussing the war which was raging with the Colonies. Being a nation of shopkeepers they talked of the conflict's mostly adverse impact on their respective businesses. The volume of the talk had aroused the interest of a group of university professors who were sitting at an adjacent table. The academics began to contribute to the discussion, talking in the soulless way of those whose learning outweighs their compassion, who see people as mere things, as pieces on a board, some things to be explained not necessarily understood.

By their talk it appeared both groups had taken much refreshment. Ill-informed opinion lit the fuse for further vitriol and injudicious, ale and wine fuelled nonsense. That was until one of them - I believe that he was an ironmonger by trade - mentioned the Royal Dockyards. The speaker was a practical man, although he was also gifted with an inciteful, argumentative tongue. He voiced some concern that the navy was stretched out like a washing line across the Atlantic, ships toing and froing keeping the army fed and supplied in a now mostly hostile country. "If" he struck the table with his open hand, a clap like thunder sending tankards and glasses scuttling for shelter "the line is cut, the army falls, and the Colonials will win." There followed a loud, vigorous exchange of views between those who felt the ironmonger was treasonous, and should apologise or be hanged (this range of views appeared to be dependent on how long the individual speaker had spent in the inn). The uproar was bubbling nicely, taunts of "traitor" and "rogue" filled the beer-soaked air, yet more voices joined in the now heated discussion.

On the fringes of the turmoil I pondered. "What if?" A question which has been the scourge of mankind through the ages, asked mostly in regret, but sometimes, as now, in hope.

Had this inn and now fevered discussion given me my cause and my purpose?

Like the moment when the voice of God called to a surprised Saul on the Damascus Road, this was the very instant at which my own mission became clear. My beer befuddled mind, the drink having its desired effect, was now once again deep in the American

Colonies, among the tree shaded paths and dappled light. My inner eye turned from the road to a fallen oak, riven with insects. Even the tallest tree can be brought low by the humble beetle. And there was I in my Deathwatch coloured coat...

Whilst deep in thought my trusty old pipe, craving but not receiving my attention, had gone out, I took a taper and lit it from a table lamp. The wax and string caught easily as though they were willingly sacrificing themselves to the hypnotic beauty of the flames. What if I were to set the ropes of the Royal Navy aflame? What would the consequences be? No ropes, no rigging, no ships, no supplies carried across the Atlantic, and for the British Army, no hope of victory.

In an unlikely setting, a drink-soaked conversation had sparked the old communion of the rebel, this rebel with his fight. I would turn the bloody fields of a far-off land back to verdant green. I had discovered that my purpose, my higher calling as some would say, was to end yet another futile and avoidable war and to save many thousands of lives on both sides. A glass or two later I left the inn to be alone with my thoughts. My dream was that within a year I would have destroyed all of the major naval dockyards. The navy would be a toothless dog, the army would have to surrender to the Colonists. I too, like Saul, would save souls.

I just had to figure out how I would do this. In my favour, I was a man no-one seemed to notice, I knew how to burgle and slip into places unseen, I knew how to draw, to plan, to procure and mix chemicals. But the compounds I was accustomed to were those which made beauty. Now I had to learn of those which would *create - at least at first - chaos and ugliness.*

Oh surely every young boy dreams of joining the army or navy and becoming an officer in the service of his country. A dashing uniform, a hero's reputation, and an ability to make ladies swoon. What more is there to life? My younger self felt at a loss when some of my fellow pupils did indeed become officers in the Army. Perhaps now was the time for redress. Although training, skill, planning, and luck are important ingredients to ensure military victory, success, when boiled down, can sometime be purely the result of logistics. If an army is not armed, supplied, and fed it will fail. By cutting the ship-borne lifeblood my actions would end the War, ensuring an overwhelming American victory, the new nation would be a beacon to the world, as my friend Thomas put it "be the cause of all mankind".

The ghosts of Roman history came forward. I would be like Fabius, the general who defeated Hannibal, not in glorious combat, the Carthaginian was far too talented to be bested in battle. Fabius defeated him in field, olive grove and orchard depriving the vast invading army of food. I would return to my newly adopted home as an officer and a hero. My commission would be granted by another country, a land freer than the one in which I was born. In my mind the church bells were already ringing for me from every steeple, accompanied by the cheers of a grateful newly forged nation."

In the deepening dark Jack was animated, proud, bright.

Chapter Seventeen

M y new, old friend's arm swept from side to side. *"It was very close to here that it all began. At that time Portsmouth saw thousands upon thousands of people and hundreds of ships come and go every year. Cargo, wood, weapons, food, drink, fuel, tar, sail, rigging, and rope flowed through and was stored around the harbour.*

In such a hive of activity there were far too many people to notice one more, so, I was able to hide in plain sight, working by day as a house painter whilst at weekends exploring, sketching, and planning. The largest structure in the Naval Dockyard was the Rope House, a monster of a building recently built-in brick following two major fires. Over three hundred yards long and twenty yards wide, it was the place where yarn was twisted into strands which were, in turn, twisted into cord or rope. Now each large ship needed something like forty miles of rope for running, rigging and hawsers. Many more miles were stowed on board to replace those cords and lines which in the harsh northern seas rotted or broke. The Rope House was stuffed with a hoard of sweet smelling oily, flammable hemp rope.

Authorities have always been disproportionately concerned with the eighth commandment. As I mentioned earlier, you could be - and many were - hanged for poaching or stealing. Security was therefore focussed on those who attempted to take things out of the Dockyard. What if someone were to bring something in, for example a Greek, or even a Scotsman, bearing a gift?

I noted that one landward gate was loosely guarded by the oldest, and most affable of night-watchmen who had a particular predilection for porter and rum which he quaffed to fortify himself against the dark and the cold.

After Portsmouth my Grand Tour continued, but unlike the gentry of the day there were no Italian cities for me, no Florence, Rome, or Naples to provide an elite education fit for a gentleman; Plymouth, Chatham, Deptford, and Woolwich were to be my future destinations. No statues, paintings, gewgaws, or encounters with exotic ladies; no ancient stories told in marble or the oils of master painters. My tour was to encompass four square towns made of brick; blood red, strong red, rectangular stones. My memories were drawn not by an old master, but by this young upstart.

But war, even of the one-man variety can be an expensive business. In October I used some of my dwindling funds to travel across the channel to Paris where I hoped to meet the American Congress representative in France, a Mister Silas Deane. I had not been at sea since my return from the Colonies. For some reason, I know not what, the lapping of the waves and the tortured cries of the gulls brought back memories of the horrors of my outbound passage. As a consequence I was unwell for the entire voyage, much to the amusement of the captain, crew and fellow passengers.

The French wanted the Americans to win partly to avenge their own defeat to the British in the Seven Years' War. As such, although they were willing to sell supplies to the American Army they had to be careful in their dealings as they did not seek to give the British grounds for declaring another expensive, bankrupting war which the French would be likely to lose. I, a simple man, walked into this labyrinth.

I had written to Mister Deane requesting a meeting, perhaps knowing it would receive short shrift I stressed my friendship with Thomas, hoping this would help to ease open the door. Indeed it did, we met at Deane's residence at the Hotel d'Entragues. I was to learn later that many others had taken the same path I now took: freedom fighters, free-loaders, Catholics, Jacobites, buccaneers, scoundrels, and other reckless young men. They had all offered to help the Colonists; most were ill equipped to do so. I was therefore one of many although the others were undoubtedly better presented, and back then, told a better tale than I could.

There are those who in the blink of an eye you know you can trust with your life and there are those which you forever doubt but have no option but to trust. Silas Deane was the sort of man who looked as though he could be killed by a sprinkle of salt. I however had no option. He met me with the fixed smile and shallow eyes of a diplomat whose mind, words and conscience have only a passing acquaintance with one another.

At first there was disbelief, but as I explained my scheme, the simplicity, the daring, and the rapid actions one dockyard followed by another two days later, then another by the end of the same week, he was won over. His eyes, initially dull and reticent, began to sparkle at the prospect of my success and as a consequence, an American victory.

In all, we met twice, I was gifted a passport - signed by the French Minister for Foreign Affairs no less! - some trivial money for my expenses and to fund my campaign a promissory note for three hundred pounds.

The wind was at my back. My course was set. I returned to England."

Chapter Eighteen

In my befuddled state, I did not fully understand Jack's intentions, so, I asked him to clarify. He obliged. *"My plan to attack Portsmouth was simple - start fires all over the town. Incendiary devices would be set in two locations, timed by their fuse length to go off at intervals. This would ensure that the fire engines were engaged elsewhere before I would then set fire to the Rope House in the Naval Dockyard. As, there were no existing devices which could fulfil my needs, my revolutionary necessity became the mother of my invention.*

I decided that I would repurpose a simple common or garden lantern, I therefore read all that I could lay my hands on about lamp design. Posing as the representative of a well-heeled customer I talked at length with silversmiths, and tinsmiths about wicks, types of oil, brightness, heat, and ways of limiting the tell-tale plumes of dark smoke.

It took a little while to perfect my design; a tin plate canister ten inches high, three and three quarter inches wide and three inches deep. It was quite unobtrusive, it looked commonplace, and could pass for a lantern, albeit one that was slightly misshapen. In Canterbury, en route to Chatham, but well away from any of my potential targets, my design became reality through the efforts of William Teach, a well-respected craftsman and tinsmith of the town. I convinced him that I was a travelling salesman with a need for a compact travelling lamp. I later regretted being quite so convincing as, sensing a profit, he took careful note of the design, no doubt intending to manufacture and sell many more. Now it may sound somewhat odd, but when I first set my eyes, and placed my hands on my own bringers of light, my Helios, there was a shiver of excitement. I felt then that these lamps and their flames of liberty would indeed light the world.

My sketchbook appeared once again in Chatham as I added yet more notes to my plan, paying particular attention this time to gates, guard rosters, and where exactly dock workers, or those purporting to be the same, could obtain access.

Although I did not wish to kill, my plan had to succeed, and I needed to protect myself or warn off, or indeed as a last resort, silence anyone who detected me. I bought pistols in London. Armed and in possession of my incendiaries and the saltpetre and turpentine needed to prime them, I set out for Portsmouth.

There I sought lodgings in an area busy enough not to notice a stranger but quiet enough where I could go about my business unhindered. As I would head north on the London road once the act was done, I chose lodgings in Barrack Street with Mr. and Mrs. Boxall, a kindly, elderly couple.

The end of the war was in sight, I just needed to keep my nerve. A tavern and beer steadied me. Tomorrow was the day.

It was early December and Portsmouth was thrumming with ships of the fleet that had returned to port to miss the worst of the winter weather and be repaired to sail afresh in the spring. Everywhere there was talk of the war, how it would soon be over, and how the Colonists would be made to pay for their treachery.

I had timed how long it would take to travel from the locations where I planned to plant my devices. This I did in both the wet and the dry, at the same time of day as when I planned to set light to the Rope House. However" Jack sighed "*the population of a port is not a constant, it ebbs and flows with the coming and going of ships. An incoming ship would be welcomed by those seeking to unload, trade or store its cargo. The sailors would also be welcomed, by family, friends or those keen to relieve the mariners of their newly earned pay. Although the walls were plastered with bills advertising these comings and goings, I was so blinkered and caught up in my own plans that I did not notice that a large merchant vessel, I cannot recall its name, was scheduled to arrive in the Harbour on the day of my action.*

There were to be two diversionary fires, these were set to draw the fire-tenders away from the Dockyard. Although, and I would say this, my devices were a wonderful design, what I had not factored in was the need for careful setting and alignment. In the throng of Eastney (the busiest part of the town) it was impossible to find a quiet spot. People sprang from each and every corner and doorway, and at times it seemed as through the walls themselves were shouting, fighting, selling, and playing, there was no peace. In desperation I entered a church where, upon removing my hat, it almost felt as if the stained-glass saints burned my skin. No matter, I had no time then for guilt or remorse. As if in prayer I kneeled, then set and arranged device number one. Unfortunately, some turpentine spilled onto my breeches and then onto the stone floor. As I moved towards the exit the pine like smell leaped towards the nose of a nearby grand dame, who was kneeling, intoning her prayers. She shrieked in alarm, extended a wizened arm and a withering look, and I ran. Red faced and sweat covered I retreated close to my lodgings in Barrack Street where I set about placing the second of my devices which would spark another diversionary fire amongst the old, dilapidated buildings thereabouts.

As the first of my two devices caught light and filled the town with panic I made my way towards the greater prize. But the crowded roads delayed my passage. The clanging bells of St. George's Church, and others on the Gosport side, mocked me as they counted the hours and the unravelling of my plan. I ran, weaving, careering, lolloping towards the Dockyard. Person, cart, and creature interrupted every stride as they looked only to their own feet, not caring for the path of others yet cursing when shoulders brushed or legs met. One particular gentleman took more than verbal offence and grabbed me by my shoulders, as he pulled back his large fist, I kicked out at his tender parts. He screamed, he cursed, I fled.

For some of us our guilt is the first thing we see when we look out through our own eyes; we therefore expect others to see it also. Particularly when those others are decked in soldier scarlet or naval blue. If captured I was doubly damned as both a deserter - aye that sword hung over my head - and as a revolutionary. I tried to calm my twittering mind, I was an invisible man who had disappeared many times before, I could and would not be remembered amongst the throng. In my own mind, I had become like water. I was able to go anywhere I wanted to, nothing could stand against me. Water is patient as it drips and wears away stone, if it cannot penetrate an object, it goes around it. Liquid seeps and creeps. Approaching my target, the throng having dispersed, I crept. It was nearing twilight as I entered the Rope House; dark was crawling through it throwing deep shadows into every nook and cranny. Workers were leaving through the far door, their footsteps clipped and clopped as they wished one another "Farewell" or "Good night." Now empty, it was as though the entire building was peering at me, windows hunched over beams as though trying to get a better look at their Angel of Death. In peace I set my three devices, flint struck metal as I lit the fuses, opening the vents to allow just the right amount of air to enter the chambers, I placed them down gently, as though they were fledgling birds, nesting them in the coils of the smaller ropes. The dry scent of fire catapulted me back to me father's forge. Light reflected on my skin, flames danced across my eyes. Seventeen years since his passing, but, in that moment we were together once again. He, a maker of horseshoes, tools, and plough shares. Me, his son, now a bringer of hope. As the flames sputtered, I prayed for my father to be at rest, and for him to be proud of his wayward son.

From my childhood memory I mustered a Bible verse, Psalm 46:

"He makes wars cease
to the ends of the earth.
He breaks the bow and shatters the spear;
he burns the shields with fire ."

It was time for me to depart."

Chapter Nineteen

"*Portsea is an island which then had one bridge joining it to the mainland. My work done, I headed north towards the bridge reaching Buckland as the church clock chimed half past four. My hurried stride caught the attention of the kind-eyed Anne Hopkins who offered me a lift in her cart which I gratefully accepted. She asked why I hurried "An ill aunt" I replied. She nodded before twitching the reins. We spoke in the stilted way of strangers. We soon stopped at Cosham at the hill overlooking the full sweep of the magnificent harbour, to the left, on the land smoke rose from the distant Dockyard, noise carried on the onshore breeze, there was the ringing of alarm bells in response to the glorious, rising, flickering of fire!*

If I were to stay in the company of a stranger there was every chance I would - because my action dominated every thought, breath, blink, and heartbeat - reveal my culpability. Making my excuses, I jumped from the cart and then once out of its sight, I ran......

The London Road swept up over Portsdown Hill, and then between a long stretch of wild woods. Through mud, stinging rain, and slicing hail I ran, then stumbled north past Petersfield, twenty miles behind me. My pace slowed as the night closed in around me, I climbed the long, slow hill to the eerie scooped earth of the Devil's Punchbowl with its crow murdered gibbet high on the skyline. It was a place I had passed many times, it was never empty of sacrifices. The wind whistled through the rotting flesh of the dead as though serenading the living with their crimes.

From the Downs towards Guildford I stumbled unceasing my legs powered as though by some infernal steam contraption. My arms pumping like a blacksmith's hammer. In the morning light, coaches passed me, their springs creaking, wheels crunching, the muzzles of the fettered horses showering me with disdain. The road was infested with yet more gibbets full of the dead. Many of the wooden frames had been attacked by the macabre human woodworm which cut off slivers to cure ailments of every kind, except perhaps gullibility. Is a place necessarily safer where more of its inhabitants have been executed? An interesting debate, but perhaps one for another time. With more and more miles behind me I had become exhilaration itself with no room for hunger, thirst, or fatigue. Perhaps blessed by Aeolus himself, I seemed to have been lifted up. I was the wind rushing towards London, and the next chapter of my great history.

It was in Kingston, by the father river Thames, where I was still for the first time in hours. My back lay on the cool grass. Night was closing in. It had been nearly two days since I had set Portsmouth ablaze. A man not suited for the intellectual rigours of university, or for a commission in the army, a man whose only use to society was as a house painter was about to bring the Royal Navy to its knees.

I now needed to break it in two, for this I needed the money which had been promised. I headed to Downing Street."

"Oh, yes" I replied, "the residence of the Prime Minister, but why on earth did you go there?"

Flash-quick Jack responded *"You may recall that Silas Deane had given me a promissory note for three hundred pounds which I was to present and draw upon in the event of my initial success. Well, the source of the money was in London. I arrived in the city I had left a few short years before, as news was reaching it of the events in Portsmouth.*

News travels fast, bad news quickest. Alerted by military despatch riders, guards had been doubled on official buildings, people huddled nervously together on street corners. The air was thick, London's smog multiplied by a sense of dread.

Not far from the river, and close by the Houses of Parliament which squatted uneasily by the Thames like a flea ridden fox, was a pretty if rather unassuming street. Summoning up my courage, and my full - if limited - height, I knocked at number four. There was a slight delay before a be-wigged servant answered the door with an air of authority and distain that only comes from years of prolonged exposure to the nobility. "Yes" he sneered "what can I do for you?" the door closing slightly with each syllable, as his eyes scanned and scowled over the length of my body. "I am here to see Mister Edward Bancroft." "Your business?" came the tart reply. "A certain Mister Deane sent me." The be-wigged one's eyes opened a little. "Certainly, Sir" the sneer had abated "please do come in," And then the strangest thing, the servant looked out of the door, left and then right, before taking my battered hat and rustic cane and showing me to the drawing room.

Deane had told me that Bancroft was sympathetic to our cause, and that he would be receptive to my plan. He listened attentively, enraptured you might say to most of my tale of daring do, and the destruction I wrought in Portsmouth. He applauded my efforts, although perhaps in my tired and heady state, I sensed an ironic, condescending tone to his voice. This I was prepared for, after all a member of the nobility would rarely speak to the likes of me, and when they did it would always be with a haughty air and an expression that they would prefer to be anywhere else, and smelling much sweeter air. When I explained, in some detail, what I had done, how I had funded the attack and my need for additional money to continue the campaign, he shook his head almost before my request had been made. "Unfortunately, Sir" more condescension "I am afraid that Mister Deane misrepresented me" with the last word emphasised as though he were some almighty being. "I will not fund your foolhardy escapade, the risks are too great. You are ill equipped for what you seek to do. You have no experience man, you are a mere…" although his words stopped his eyes continued speaking - a painter, a Scotsman, a… "and as such you are bound to fail." With that he rose, and dismissed me. I protested, arguing that the only thing with which I was ill equipped was money, something he could very easily remedy. I then explained in a low voice as he showed me to the door, the benefits to all of an early end to the war, not just the lives saved, but something far more important to him and his kind - the benefit to trade. He softened a little, there was a scintilla of self-doubt, he then - perhaps to ease me through the exit - agreed to a second meeting the following day. This would give him time, he said, to consider his options. My hope hung by a fraying thread, I prayed that the night would bring him purpose and strength.

Coaches and riders were bringing more news from Portsmouth.

As I had seen from Portsdown Hill, the fire in the Rope House had taken hold, but thousands of sailors, marines and dockyard workers had worked to fight the fire. Reports talked of the great line of buckets which passed through the streets, a snake with the sea at its tail, and flames at its mouth. The same reports spoke of axes and saws which cut and bit into burning beams to free them, and stop the spread of fire. Every one of the newspapers celebrated the hero of the hour, James Gambier. Some middle ranking officer, but surely destined for greater things, who had averted disaster by ordering his ship, the brig The Albion, which was carrying 2,000 barrels of gunpowder, to put to sea where it would be out of harm's way. All of London's coffee shops and taverns were full of rumour. Surely, the most common one ran, this must have been an unprovoked attack by the cowardly French, shattering the fragile peace. "We must and we should declare war" was the refrain on every "patriot's" lips. Sadly, talk of wars to be waged always comes easy to some.

It was against this background, that, in the midst of the bustle of Charing Cross, in the Salopian Coffee House, I next met Bancroft. Although the Salopian was a hive of activity with comings and goings; there seemed to be a more cautious tone than usual to the conversations. Everyone seemed to be listening not just to their colleagues or friends, but to all other chatter as though hearkening for talk of plots and plotters. Faces which were probably never truly warm had developed a flintiness, as though willing to scream "traitor" at the least possible provocation.

At first, I did not recognise Bancroft. It was as though he had deliberately chosen a coat and hat to camouflage him amongst the dark wood. I was seated, he slithered towards me before whispering, putting me in mind of Eve and apples. "I have been mulling over our discussion" he began, each syllable less audible than the last as though he was a deflating balloon, "and have decided not to support your venture." To any listening ear this would have given the impression of a merchant or entrepreneur deciding not to progress with a risky voyage. "Why sir?" I responded, equally veiled "the return on a small investment could be significant, and opportunities such as this are rare indeed."

There was a slight growl in his voice "But this venture Sir, is not that of a gentleman. Your proposal is more suited to a rogue, and I Sir have my honour, whereas you…" He left the sentence unfinished, perhaps concerned about what this particular ruffian would do. I opened my mouth to disagree but immediately realised that my breath could be better spent. He rose and left. Crestfallen, I gazed into the dark swirl of my coffee. So, the war I was proposing to bring to an end was a civilised one for civilised men! By striking at things and places I was not playing their game. The one where two armies of soldiers assemble and take shot after shot at each other, until whoever has fewer dead or more alive when the muskets stop is proclaimed the victor? I, the one who intended to end this slaughter was the barbarian?!

I had sought help from both the French and the Americans, but my enemy's enemies were not my friends. All of Europe was fettered by the same tyranny, of gentlemen who could not see the future. After another coffee I resolved then and there that I would act alone.

A few days later the Navy opened an investigation into the fire. My near nemesis The Bow Street Runners were dispatched to carry out the task. They questioned all those they could identify who were in the vicinity of the Rope House on the evening of the attack. Their preliminary findings, as reported in the columns of the press, concluded that they were "unable to ascertain whether the misfortune arose from accident or design" although they soon sought "to find and arrest several suspicious persons that are imagined to have had some hand in setting fire to the dockyard." I permitted myself a congratulatory smile as I read the newspaper coverage, there was no mention of an unassuming Scottish man. There are few, but some advantages to near invisibility!

Although you may not be known, you may be immortalised. The striped street corner booths with their Punch and Judy shows were soon to feature a character which bore a close and unsettling resemblance to myself. "Brimstone" an evil character with a wicked laugh and a flaming torch soon replaced the Devil as Mr. Punch's chief adversary. The puppet hero had managed where the incompetent, slapstick Bow Street Runners had not, to track down Brimstone to his subterranean lair. Punch wrestled with the villain, seemingly succumbing to the villain's stranglehold before eventually overcoming Brimstone to a chorus of cheers from the audience.

It could have been my imagination, but did Punch look directly at me as he cursed the now dead Brimstone? Did Punch's swazzled voice call my name? Would Bancroft or indeed Mr. Punch himself reveal my identity to the authorities?

Sensing another net closing, it was time once again for me to leave London."

Jack was now still, his earlier animation gone. He was wrapped up in his memories. I too had felt compelled to leave the capital. It was a place we had both never learned to love.

Chapter Twenty

I sensed that Jack had perhaps never before told anyone his full story, there was too much effort in his recall, no well-formed phrases or familiar words. He took a deep breath before continuing.

"Having shared my plan with Bancroft I was concerned that he would in turn share it with the authorities. To continue my attacks on the naval dockyards could be reckless. I changed my plan, my path now headed west from London through the grey-green frosted fields of the shire counties towards Bristol. With the passing of each day I further added to my long list of misdemeanours, I borrowed without the owners' consent food, money and once a recalcitrant horse although the creature soon forcibly discarded me when it realised that I was terrified of it.

If Portsmouth was defined by its military power, Bristol, then the second city of the land, was the war chest which thronged with ships bearing the plunder from slavery and its works. My experience in the Colonies, where I was, for a short while, almost a white slave filled me with hatred for the vile trade. Ships on the middle passage between West Africa and America would typically lose one third or more of their human cargo, a loss treated with no more gravity than if it were tainted wine! I vowed that those who profited from the trafficking of human beings should be made to pay.

On my way westward somewhere in the Cotswolds among the honey stone and sheep-fat market towns I met John. There was an energy about him. He was a firebrand, quite like Tom in some ways, but he taught not of the rights of Man, but of the right of God and duties of man. His Bible was permanently either clasped to his heart, or held open to preach. His words were not the grandiloquent of the pulpit but were those of the common man. We talked by a well as we drew water, he because Adam's Ale was all he ever drank, whereas I that day could afford nothing stronger. We talked of our lives, deeply, in the way passing strangers often do, without the prospect of future meetings the tongue is loosened. He too was a rebel of sorts, and was not shocked with my tales of desertion and theft - I skipped over some of my other sins - sparing the blushes of this Godly man. I told him of the slave market, the plantation, of the cruelty which printed money. I also told him of the promise of hope I had seen in America. In turn, he told me of his own hopes and dreams, of building a new Jerusalem where all men could be free, where there was no slavery of mind or body, and his own philosophy, his rule of life, which he offered to me:

"Do all the good you can,
By all the means you can,
In all the ways you can,
In all the places you can,
At all the times you can,
To all the people you can,
As long as ever you can."

John had his dreams, but the world needs its dreamers. He too was headed towards Bristol, a place - in his words - where "People devoted themselves not just to making money, but to the love of it.

Making idols out of gold."

What first struck me about the city was there was no gaiety or politeness. It seemed that all were in a hurry running, loading, and unloading the trade of many nations, and that responsibility, that weight of commerce had formed lined, cloudy, care worn faces. Perhaps their obsession with money had made them care for nobody but themselves, or if they did, it was purely transactional, as a tool for the pursuit of gain, whatever or whoever the cost.

Clifton sat high above the river, stately white stone houses peering cautiously, coquettishly at what happened below. Gaze filtered by curtain and window blind. But the stench of death rises, always, eventually catching in the throat of the perpetrator. The great men of the town whose houses were built on the spoils of the middle passage, taking once freemen, women, and children westward towards woe. Poor unfortunates, who were captured, shipped, enslaved, and then forced to work until death. Many fortunes sat in the grand houses above the town, and of course behind every great fortune lurks a greater crime.

In the run up to the feast of Christmas, with its gluttony and occasional calculated charity, the town was full of many poor men seeking work on the docks and in the warehouses, which sat like drunk dominoes leaning on and into one another. How could I damage the war chest as well as striking a blow against those who had grown rich on the suffering of others? In the dark, crowded, sinister streets my thoughts turned to my next attack. As unobtrusively as possible I watched, sketched, and plotted. I sought my first lodging, cheap and close to the port where I would scratch onto paper my record of the gates, the location and number of guards, and what cargo was openly or perhaps secretly stored where.

The poorly printed sheets pasted on walls announced auctions, plays, ship sailings, hangings, and men wanted, They also shouted of rewards being offered for information leading to the arrest and conviction of those responsible for the Portsmouth Fire. The authorities perhaps thought that within the warren of wooden houses and the menagerie of miscreants there would be at least one who would know the perpetrator. Guilt is the strangest of feelings. As I mentioned a few minutes past even though no one could possibly know you were the person responsible, every look, every gaze directed towards you appears to see through to your very soul, like sunlight reflected through a bottle, burning. It is as though your crimes are written on your very face with each line and shadow bearing the trace of iron gall ink etched by the pen of the all-seeing onto the parchment of your skin. Fearing discovery, I kept moving, never more than two nights in any lodging house, I trod the fine line between sociability and keeping everything of myself close and closed. I did what I could not to stand out. I even tried to change my appearance with a haircut and to change my voice with a new less obviously Scottish accent. I failed. My talent for mimicry was always limited, even at school when the other boys would appropriate the voices and mannerisms of the teachers I could not. I was only ever able to be me.

I continued to work on my infernal devices, my very own metaphorical hammer, as a result of which everything which *floated or docked now looked like a nail. My incendiaries - my "Vulcans" ready to exact vengeance on the English politicians who believed themselves to be Mars the god of war - were now simply balls of resin and pitch. They were easy to make from ingredients which were readily available to the many faceless, interchangeable, itinerant tradesman: painters, boatwrights and carpenters, who worked in such a large city.*

By Crane Number 3 on Bristol Quay there were three merchantmen whose decks and holds were filled with the vile instruments - the irons and shackles - of slavery, The Savanna la Mer, The Hibernian, and The Fame.

Close by the ships, poorly lit, and huddled together, Quay Lane and nearby Bell Lane were rich with warehouses full from the profits of the nefarious wicked triangle which took woollen cloth, tools, pots of iron & brass and weapons to Africa where they were exchanged for enslaved humans. These poor souls were then transported to the West Indies or to North America where they were sold to work on plantations. The slavers' blood money was used to buy tobacco, sugar, coffee, and rum which flowed back to Bristol from which it spread feeding the addictions of all. Like a vile heart pumping evil around a rotten world.

My plan, which had taken almost a month to mature, was that the three merchant ships, their cargoes and the contents of the nearby warehouses would all burn bright on the night of the 19th of January. But sadly, only one warehouse full of grain and Spanish wool (not the rum I had been led to believe) was destroyed. Some of my devices elsewhere were discovered before they could flame righteously. Soon, there was a realisation that if fortune had not intervened, the whole shame-soaked city may have been greatly damaged, punished by a purifying fire.

The Mayor and Council were in panic. They called upon the Government to send troops, so three companies of His Majesty's finest dragoons were dispatched. Rumours ran, jumped, and climbed. No one man could ignite or attempt to light so many fires in so many different places, surely this must be the work of an organised group. Some classical scholars spoke of a modern-day Catilinarian conspiracy. Was the city being burned to destroy banking and trade records and therefore cancel debts? Major creditors immediately became suspects. But not I who was never rich enough to borrow, I started with nothing, most of which I still owned.

Day and night patrols were organised in every parish, every stranger was under suspicion and the entire city became a tinderbox of distrust and accusation. Once again, The Bow Street Runners were dispatched to chase my shadow. It was in late January, just after the eclipse of the sun which some took as portentous, that the Navy Board issued a description of me given to them by workers in the Dockyard. Although vague, it and the £50 reward – enough to feed a family for a year - sent an icicle though my heart. Newspapers were full of the search for "the persons responsible for burning down the Portsmouth Rope House." Although I knew that it gave me hope, and increased my chances of escape, but when I read about myself in the newspapers as someone with "nothing much to mark him out, unless it was a furtive air as he strolled along the waterfront conning the slips and the dockside warehouses," I was

171

affronted. The nation was in a panic not seen since the days when the Bonny Prince and his tartan army cut through the north en route to London, and I, the man responsible, was described as a non-entity! There were even anonymous letters sent to the Prime Minister Lord North from someone claiming responsibility for my deeds. The sheer affrontery of it!

A phantom was attacking the very heart of England. Everywhere, everyone seemed to walk more quickly, to speak more quietly, and to hurry home before dark. Streets were quieter, inns begun to serve only those they knew. Many unfortunate strangers were beaten by angry mobs for their resemblance to my ill-described shadow.

Some newspapers whispered of conspiracy, "Who would benefit from these events?" they enquired. To some there was one clear answer, the Colonial Secretary and staunch opponent of American Independence, Lord Germain who had his sight set on the highest office in the land. By creating havoc and positioning himself as the only one able to deal with it, he would undermine those in charge, and rise to fill the vacuum. Soon, there was another act of Parliament, the American High Treason Bill. Perhaps triggered by this, or by the relentless newspaper coverage, people began to recall more about me than my shadow. The colour of my coat, my blank face – perhaps nothing there to worry me, as both could be changed or disguised.

But there was one thing one of the dockworkers recalled; my gait. I must admit it is not something I had ever really considered. Yes, my family and I tended to pitch a little from side to side as we walked. My blessed Mother described it as a sort of open, even jolly way of walking. Not something, until that point, I had ever thought of as a characteristic, but it was something which had etched itself into the eyes of witnesses. I soon became fixated by how others walked, some sure, almost mechanically, others with cat like caution, some plodded cart horse like whereas others were like malfunctioning marionettes. Each one had their own way of walking, but worryingly enough none were like my own. Thereafter I would repeatedly but surreptitiously walk by shop windows gazing at my reflection, memorising the mannerisms, then mentally sketch my limbs, seek to correct my movements, and then walk by another window. Walk, observe, correct, and repeat. Slowly, and with a great deal of mental effort, and no little discomfort, I felt that I began to exercise some control over my unruly limbs.

A few days elapsed before the reward for information leading to my capture increased to one thousand pounds - a veritable fortune - as the Mayor, the local Member of Parliament, the Society of Merchant Venturers, and other Bristol dignitaries all contributed. Unfortunately, one of my devices had failed to ignite at all and its contents: gunpowder, oil, cork, resin, turpentine, and paper were plain for all to see. The magistrates exhorted any person who had disposed or sold of any such items to provide them with information so "that the perpetrators of this horrid action may be discovered and brought to condign (suitable) punishment." Wherever there is fear there is a fortune or a reputation to be made, before long, in addition to dragoons, and Runners, there were fortune hunters, patriots and what felt like the entire nation on my trail.

The phrase "nothing to mark him out" churned, clanged, and crashed around my mind. There was an option to simply disappear. *If I was indeed so indistinct, that should prove no challenge to a man of my wit and ingenuity. I would lose any of the few characteristics that people, if and when they exerted every ounce of brain power, would recall. The russet brown coat, (although battered and torn stood out somewhat in the midst of identical cheerless shades of dark brown and priestly black), would be burned or surreptitiously swapped for another. My hair which had now grown into an unkempt mane would be tamed, it would be further trimmed and more frequently cut so that it resembled a man of substance. My shoulders which were now bowed, weighed down by the risk of discovery and burden of duty, would rise, freed from my self-imposed shackles. Yes, I could disappear…"* Jack paused, reflecting on a road not taken, *"but, I had tried and had sent the chill of fear running through the Government and what passed for a King. Unshackled I could strike again, not only to end a brutal war. I may also call time on tyranny. The monarch was not fit to rule, it was not the fact they were Hanoverians, all sovereigns rule for the benefit of themselves, their courtiers and supporters, mostly men of power and influence. The country was starving, disease was rampant, children were dying in the streets. All this while the rich prospered from slavery, from the devilish factories which had begun to blight the land and from wars in which brave young men perished."*

On that last word Jack looked straight at me, at the half-man who a few short hours ago had wanted to be even less.

Chapter Twenty One

"*Aye, but the mind is not a creature which sits quietly dog-like in a corner awaiting its master's next command. It is a restive cat, malcontent, forever pacing the room. Although I had not yet incapacitated the Navy, and stopped a senseless war, I had come within a whisker of doing so. By fading and disappearing into the half-light, my legend would grow. Walking away from Bristol through the empty, frosted, muddy cart tracks of Somerset I smiled like a simpleton at the thought that my story could be used to quieten children and send them to their beds. Mothers would threaten their unruly brood with a visit from an unnamed villain. The newspapers had not yet given me an identity. The weak sun half-heartedly coloured the western sky, the air began to nip and chill, the first pinpricks of light appeared in the night sky. Mars, Venus, Mercury and Jupiter, and then the rest of the celestial canopy which hangs above all of our heads. Groups of stars which told mythic tales. These names I had taught myself some years before when I spent a while lurking behind trees waiting for the creaking, careering coaches, the foam-flecked bridles, and the, hopefully, heavily laden passengers. Each sky-held light has a name. Across the northern hemisphere, people would gaze towards the heavens and see twins, a hunter, bears, a massive dipping plough, and the unflinching Pole Star.*

Was my destiny now northward? Was I to leave this fight behind me and return to my home town, or perhaps another place? The Americans and the perfidious French had betrayed me. Neither had seen what it was possible to do with the re-arranged articles of the everyday sprinkled with my imagination. There were undoubtedly cranks and misfits who had through the ages been drawn to a noble cause, seeking to emulate Sir Galahad or Odysseus but more like Don Quixote in their manner, talents, and achievements. Was I to be viewed through the same lens, seen as a clanking, creaking comical Spaniard even after the very near victory at Portsmouth? But those in power now knew I was a capable man, in truth so did I, even my own worst critic - my inner schoolmaster - was now silent. To know is all. If I had been supported and financed who knows what may have happened? The skies of Portsmouth, Chatham, Deptford, Woolwich, and Bristol would have filled with the smoke of rope and smouldering ships, No soldiers would set forth and no slaves would be traded for months or years. Thousands of innocents, white and black, would have been saved by my own fiery hand.

But why think on the past? I would seek oblivion and lose myself in the smoke and squalor of Birmingham or Manchester. I resolved to resume my trade as a painter in a place far away from the sea. My future was mapped. Like steam, I would rise, disappear and be forgotten.

I snuggled down in an empty barn, straw my blankets and bed. There were noises outside, but they did not prevent me sliding sweetly into sleep. Apparently, we dream every night. Well that may be true, but I remember very few of my fleeting nocturnal thoughts, and the images which played out in the theatre of my own head. That is, apart from one. On the night I resolved to disappear as smoke I was visited as I slept. He gazed at me for what seemed like an eternity, through his red-rimmed, kindly, yet challenging eyes. He then uttered a solitary word. It was the one he would use as he created from fire, as we children huddled, entranced. The word, his motto, "Eudaemonia." There was a crash of red and white-hot sparks as the hammer connected. The anvil holding firm as my father shaped the molten metal. Reflected in those eyes was no longer the light of the forge; instead there was the faintest glimmer of light from a small tin box. In the short time I knew him my father never ranted, raved, or cursed; he was a man with careful, precise actions whose expression filled eyes replaced many words. Those same eyes were ordering me, in his gentle yet firm way, to continue what I had already begun.

As the barnyard awoke around me and I sought to take my leave before I was discovered, I could think of nothing but my dream. I had survived two terrifying crossings of the Atlantic, a flight across the wilds of America, an encounter with a bear, a career as a highwayman, several desertions from His Majesty's Army and the dogged pursuit of the Bow Street Runners. All of these - and their attendant risks of drowning, disease, jaws, claws, flogging or hanging - could have killed me. They had not. Was this a coincidence, or had I been saved, for something special; more distinguished than merely vanishing into the thick air of Birmingham or Manchester?

But cows and milk maids wake earlier than most, and my shuffling in the barn was noticed by one such. She did not scream or sound an alarm, indeed she shared her meagre breakfast with me. Country folk may lack the sophistication of those who live in cities, but what they do not know of literature, fine music, or the theatre, they more than compensate for in knowledge of nature, human and otherwise.

She had borne children; seen some die and others move away. Her husband, not seen for some four years, was a sailor who she believed still lived. She prayed every night for his safe return. We shared food and talk. Sometimes a stranger can elicit more than a friend. She - her name I regret to say I forget - sensed I was in turmoil, her words then were perhaps the wisest I have heard, wiser than any Roman or Greek, Ovid excepted.

"Nobody can protect you from the fact that life will break you, it breaks us all. Nothing can protect you from that. But before it does, you have to feel there is a reason you are here on earth. Some apples fall and waste their sweetness. Do not fall before you have achieved whatever is your destiny."

She picked up her now empty breakfast cloth. "I have cows to milk, butter, and cheese to make, stomachs to fill. I need to feed my family, and stay alive until my beloved returns, that is my destiny. Know yours. Go easy, step lightly, stay free."

I resolved to continue. I may have been penniless, alone and hunted but nevertheless I was still free. I then resolved to head east towards Chatham where ships of the fleet were built and repaired. With the harsh weather in the North Atlantic ships took a battering, and with the need to continually replenish the Army they lasted less than two years between major repairs. It was mid-winter, the shipyard would be full. With attention now on Bristol and Portsmouth both of which the papers reported were bristling with soldiers, Chatham - which I had previously reconnoitred - would give me the opportunity to take the prize. I was a young man, but those of my origin or embraced profession tended to live to no more that thirty-three years. But what great things could be done in such a short span of time, indeed Alexander the Great, and Jesus Christ himself both spent that brief time on the earth. With my seven or so years left on this globe what could I achieve? As a painter I could scratch a living and slowly poison myself before being buried in a pauper's grave, stripped of anything of worth and sprinkled with sour lime. If I were to die, perhaps sometime soon, at least I would be on a path to glory.

A modern martyr, my blood would perhaps be a seed on which the world could begin anew. Strangely, I was empowered by the thought of capture, trial, and death. Although I did not seek it; I did not fear. My manifest destiny was through fire, and the burning of rope and wood, to bring peace and to slay the God of War. Though dead I would live on.

Perhaps fearful of the bogeyman now in their midst, everywhere, each village and hamlet seemed shuttered, locked tight. Doors were heavily barred and chained, and brazier-warmed watchmen stood guard on the corners of the more prosperous streets. But, if you knew where to find them there were always pickings to be had, locks could always be undone and things of value found. But each and every theft increased my risk of capture. I purloined food, drink and money in towns and villages as I journeyed east, towards the rising sun, and perhaps the dawning of my own last days.

It was in a haberdasher's shop in Calne, in the county of Wiltshire where I was searching in the dark glimmer of night for something to eat or exchange for food. I was hoping that an unknowing Samaritan's cash box would offer itself up by reflecting the moon, or some pewter would glow like a dying ember. Whilst my eyes and fingers played in the darkness searching for the faintest offering a door, which I did not feel I needed to secure, caught in a gust of wind. This witness to my presence woke the household. There was a noise on the stair. A heavy tread, there were voices, threatening and mean. I turned, left, and ran. Through the dark and fog I stumbled, the mud, ice, cart tracks and the wicked fingers of frost catching my every step. I dared not look behind towards the noise and shadows which followed me, in case I saw the red-eyed cackling Devil himself.

The road east was empty apart from the occasional farm cart, with their resigned bulls and dreary drivers. My face was scarf swaddled, so my grunts of welcome did not draw attention or unwanted conversation. We were all hurrying somewhere with no time, hoping we would reach our destination before the cold froze our bones. Some miles on, muddled by tiredness I stumbled, twisting my left ankle. My leg soon lost feeling, my fingers too were numbing. I hobbled on through the night and into the next day. At dusk, looming among the trees was a skeleton of stone. I was wet with frost, fear, and sweat, starving hungry and exhausted. Where once I was and felt bird free, I was now fearful and stalked. I collapsed in the overgrown ruins of a once great castle. I prayed that I had escaped my pursuers, but as I could not take another step, I did not know whether these ancient battlements would be my protection, or my prison."

Chapter Twenty Two

"*It was sometime later, when from one of the many who insisted on talking to, or with, me that I learned that this very castle in the hills of Hampshire, on the outskirts of Odiham, had been home to the rebellious baron Simon de Montfort who had led an almost successful insurrection against an unpopular king. It was also the home for eleven years to another troublesome Scot, King David the Second. They say that history repeats, but I did not expect to stay in this place for as long as my compatriot!*

The morning mist delivered an unexpected guest in the form of the heavy-treaded haberdasher who in his dogged pursuit of me had gathered a small troop. I was soon accommodated in the warm welcoming straw of the Odiham House of Correction, otherwise known as the Bridewell. Perhaps so named by a man who had the misfortune to be unlucky in marriage. After so much time fleeing, foraging, and flinching at every approaching noise or shadow it was a strangely restful place; thick walls around you can sometimes be a comfort. The keeper, a ruddy faced man, with an accent so thick you could have ploughed it, was kindness personified.

After several hunger wracked days, the beer, bread, and cheese were a veritable feast. My ankle poulticed and bandaged I drifted into sleep. I woke to discover that I had been charged with (I expected as litany) …attempted theft, the only crime of which I was accused being my last. In a state of disbelief, but sensing an opportunity to be free, I began to negotiate with the constable offering my pair of pistols to the claimant along with a fulsome apology as recompense for any loss or damage caused. The haberdasher, sensing a significant profit on the proposed deal, seemed keen to drop charges and reach an agreement. All was going well until the keeper laid out all of my possessions in public view. Besides the pistol there was nothing of note besides a lantern shaped cannister, a horn of powder, my pistols, and a bottle of turpentine. Nothing to attract too much attention, my transaction with the haberdasher was reaching a successful conclusion, and freedom beckoned. I hoped another apology together with some justification for my action would help to bring matters to a close.

"Thank you gentlemen for your forgiveness. I would like to apologise for the considerable inconvenience I realise I have caused. I thought I heard someone breaking into the shop, and I tried to apprehend them. I see how my actions then and subsequently could have been misinterpreted. But I took nothing and caused no damage. Good day."

All parties were content. I raised my hat and was just about to take my remaining possessions and my leave when a rider arrived fresh with the latest newspapers and notices. The crowd's attention soon turned to the papers which were being handed around, surely there was nothing to worry me here. Refreshed and reinvigorated I would soon be stepping albeit slowly and carefully towards Chatham. The keeper was engaged in discussion, I did not want to incur his wrath by leaving without his approval. I gazed upon the fine houses of the pretty town while I waited.

"To the side if you please" a barked voice broke my reverie. The barker's head twitched from the newly arrived paper to the items

in my hands. A wide triumphal smile split his face "We have found the arsonist!"

Some while later I was awakened by z-zum, z-zum, z-zum; the sound of a heavy stick on prison bars. There were perhaps a hundred faces peering at me, it was like a scene from a Breugel painting. They had apparently all paid the keeper a shilling to see the infamous prisoner. They shouted a whole range of questions at me, as well as a range of expletives, some of which I had not heard before, which just goes to show there is always something new to learn. I was thankful that the impenetrable accent of these south-country folk prevented some of the fouler curses from reaching my understanding. I obviously answered nothing, not confirming, or denying anything at all. The crowd soon grew restless, and I sensed some begrudged their shilling although others may have felt that my silence only added to my air of mystery and menace.

It was not long before the King's Messenger, a Mr. Randall, arrived in a shower of bewigged efficiency, two Bow Street Runners accompanied him - one of whom I am sure I recognised from the Devil Tavern - I was placed in a set of manacles I was to become quite attached to over the coming days.

The New Prison at Clerkenwell was the next stop on my own grand tour.

Sir John Fielding himself met this particular piece of refuse every day for the next month. Why do those who purport to be intelligent ask such inane questions? Did they think they were talking to some numbskull who would willingly incriminate themself? A grammar school education is a wonderful thing, as I am sure you know yourself Will; it prepares you, should you wish to use it in such a manner, to be extremely irksome and obstinate.

I was not betrayed by my own tongue, but by one of my canisters which was recognised - from the description in the newspapers - by my landlady in Portsmouth, Mrs. Boxall had obviously gone through my belongings while I was out. I resolved never again to trust a woman from Portsmouth. Soon, the trickle of evidence became a flood as other witnesses came forward. By the end of the month Sir John was able to point his tottering finger at me, and assert in his tremulous voice, in the tone rehearsed for his great condemnations, that I was the villainous, newspaper-christened John the Painter.

Flocks of the curious descended on the prison to see the latest in a long line of rogues. Me and my kind were there to be gawped at by well-heeled entertainment seekers. Fellow prisoners tried to engage me in conversation, perhaps seeking bragging rights so they may boast that they had spent time in the company of the great villain, the most wanted, the incendiary John the Painter. I spoke with some, my tongue a little loosened by their kind gifts of Portuguese wine.

It was clear that, although a trial had not yet begun, based on the evidence of an ever growing number of witnesses I would most likely hang.

What would the story be that was told of me? Of a rebel with no cause, of a mere mercenary driven - like many more in history - by nothing more than a love of gold? If that were to be my story, I would pass into history as nothing of substance, merely the tool of the enemy with naught to tell of my own will, my own conscience, or my own war. My tale needed to be told. I was weakening by the day. Little food had passed my lips whilst in prison. It was as though I had forgotten how to be hungry, although it was also because I had heard tell that a hungry man is able to endure torture - a threat which loitered in the dark corners of the eyes of my captors - more ably than a well fed one. On my last night, in that prison, I was visited by Thomas Lawrence, after a few glasses of fine French wine, I swore that he would be the one to tell my story. My dying confession would tell the truth no newspaper had even guessed at, it would tell of my ambition, and how I had come within a sliver of achieving it. Of the tens of thousands who would no doubt buy Lawrence's pamphlet, most would jeer at my defeated wretchedness, some however may take up my baton, and carry on the fight..."

Of course it was a trick of the light, how could it be anything else? But as Jack spoke, as his story took shape, so did he. No longer just shadow but substance. Are we all just stories who disappear when not told? My new friend continued.

Chapter Twenty Three

"As my offence was committed in the county of Hampshire my trial took place in Winchester. I was transported there in a coach which rolled like a ship in an Atlantic storm as it drove west through the rutted roads. I was squeezed in with three foul-smelling soldiers, whose tricornered hats scuffed the roof and whose tunics were frayed, splattered with beer and dirt. It is so very difficult to take authority seriously when, at close quarters, it looks so ridiculous.

My eyes scanned the thickets and spinneys for signs of a daring highwayman - even one of the stuttering Scottish kind - to rescue me from my predicament, but there is never one around, when you most need it...

The horses pulled this precious cargo towards the capital of Ancient England, and the home of the headstrong St. Swithun who objected to his indoor shrine, preferring to be subject to the feet of passers-by and to the raindrops pouring from on high.

At points along the route gawpers gathered, yet more folks who I disappointed with my blank, sunken expression when they expected howls of rage, flights of oratory or at the very least an acknowledging wave. I later overheard one of the guards say that the countryfolk all agreed that because of my poor manners I deserved to hang.

We arrived in Winchester later the same day, I was sixty-five miles closer to eternity. The trial took place the very next day in the Great Hall.

As the night faded the surrounding streets filled with an almighty throng. A vast crush of folk pushed their way through when the doors opened at a quarter past seven. As the great bells pealed eight the crowd hushed as the two judges - William Ashurst and Beaumont Hotham - sat on the throne-like dais beneath a replica of King Arthur's round table. Did the spirits of the knights of legend: Gawain, Lancelot, Galahad, Percivale, Lionell, Bedivere, Palomedes, Lamorak, Pelleas, Kay and their mighty king look down at me? Did they also sit in judgement? It then dawned on me that amongst all of the heroism and chivalry there is one knight, Mordred, who would bring Camelot crashing down. Dull light filtered through the arched windows which were stained with the stained-glass shields and symbols of sycophants and skulduggers. Who of these I wondered were themselves also treacherous sons?

Removed of all of its trappings, how would justice sound? If stripped of the obtuse and impenetrable language would it merely sound like an empty vessel or a clanging gong? A bewigged pantomime began to surround me. There would be, could be, only one outcome, but I had known fear for too long since my first stuttering "Halt!" to feel its grip now.

Light-headed, it was as though I rose from my very body and sat with legs swinging like a schoolboy on a crossbeam by one of the shining painted suns. From my vantage point I saw that judges Ashurst's and Hotham's expensive clothes were threadbare, their horsehair wigs piebald. I saw that the judges dozed repeatedly and I also saw the Jury barely concealing their admiration for the eloquence of the prosecution, some even applauding as though at the theatre. I also saw how stories, even those as gripping and dramatic as my own, bored and tired many. Snores, yawns, and grumbles filled the benches, where bread and cheese were scoffed, and strong drink passed many lips.

I was surprised at the length of the trial, seven whole hours, when most trials back then even those for capital offences took a matter of minutes. The well-fed, the well-bred, the well-read, the well dressed, the well to-do, and the well-connected, oh, they were all arrayed against me. There was no lawyer engaged in my defence, which was standard practice at the time, Liberty had lost her scales. There were however five prosecutors, led by a William Davy and including three other barristers John Fielding (who was nephew of Sir John, and included purely on merit…), Francis Buller, Thomas Missing (the ancient Lord Chief Justice), and Lord Mansfield. It struck me that the government were taking every precaution to ensure they did not slip up, and allow this particular phantom to escape.

Although massively outnumbered by the finest legal minds of the land, and outgunned by their knowledge of protocol, precedent, and punishment, I did not permit myself to be cowed. Notwithstanding the exhaustion of mind and body, and the intense pain of my left leg which had not yet recovered from its twisting on a frost-kissed road, I mustered my defence, inspired by the nearby legendary knights who had given their own lives for an ideal. Words about freedom, justice, and peace. I coolly declared myself to be "Not guilty." The judges glared at me as though I were merely a small self-important dog whining in the dark and keeping its betters awake.

As the hours passed the accusations mounted so that they appeared to totter beside me; leaning, lurching, and leering as words took substance. I gazed at the grandeur all around me when my eyes alighted on the golden lion and unicorn atop the Judge's dais. The lion has been hurriedly crafted by someone who has obviously never seen a live beast or even a well-executed picture of one, but must have been told what one looked like in an inn late at night. The unicorn however appeared to be so well formed - for a mythical beast - that it bore the scars of reality. The horn was wonderfully twisted, pointing left as though its owner carelessly galloped at full speed into a wall, which may well have explained the grotesque mouth, teeth bared smiling lopsidedly at the Court.

Inspired by the ludicrous surroundings, the mythical creatures, the counterfeit round table and spurred on by the knowledge that it is not the size of the dog in the fight that matters, but the size of the fight in the dog, I punched back with my questions. If I were to die, and let me be frank, at no point did I feel this was anything but a foregone conclusion, I would go down swinging. Oh, please pardon my gallows humour. Oh they did their very best to bait this bear, but it, I, snarled, scratched and bit as long as I was able to stand.

The case against me was remarkably slim, the fundamental question asked by the prosecution being whether an innocent man would carry about his person a powder horn of gunpowder and a full tinderbox? This circumstantial evidence was woven together with half-recalled memories of my being seen in one place or another. Nineteen witnesses were called to give evidence against me. I, imprisoned and penniless with no counsel of my own was, *needless to say, unable to track down and request the appearance of those who may have helped my case.*

I did of course question the veracity of those called to testify against me. Although my heart pounded, I spoke clearly and precisely, my stutter had not accompanied me from the cells. "The witnesses here assembled cannot, with any accuracy recall dates and times, which are crucial I would suggest if you were assembling a case. They all seem to believe that they have seen me in the shadows. But I, I, I – my voice rising - am a freeborn man, not a mere absence of light."

Recognising the relatively weak case against me, and the demand from the King himself that I be convicted, the prosecution focused on using my own words against me. Whilst in prison I had been befriended by John Baldwin, an American painter who quietly professed his own revolutionary sympathies. Bored, and befuddled by wine over several evenings, believing I was confiding in a fellow traveller, I told Baldwin my story.

My "friend" stood before me, in the dock, using my own words as weapons. I was enraged declaring:

"I remark to the witness that this is a righteous Judge, who also giveth righteous judgement; so, beware of what you say Mr. Baldwin, perjure not yourself, you are in the sight of God, as is all of this company." Baldwin did not dare to look at me.

"Mr. Baldwin" I continued "the words I spoke to you when we met, and took strong wine together, could of course all be fiction. I delight in words and the telling of stories. I sensed you were not the person you purported to be, so I may have led you a merry dance

like Chaucer's Miller."

Baldwin turned pale. The crowd cried out in disbelief. The Judge attempted to restore a semblance of order. In the grumbling silence I asked his lordship.

"Whose authority do you have sir?"

"That of His Majesty the King" came the lofty reply.

Perhaps I should have held my tongue, but I did not. "Ah, yes, the Hanoverian Madman" a pause which allowed my seditious words to seep into the ears of the crowded room, I continued "the King" I almost spat that word "who will go down in history as the one who lost American Colonies."

Uproar inevitably followed. The crowd all glared as though I was some rare and exotic creature. They pointed, shouted and cursed. They were barely able to control themselves, it was as though I were in the public gardens, some ape behind twisted wire. As the Judges retired to consider the case the noise rose to a crescendo. Amongst the hubbub, mumble, and rhubarb there were howls, shouts, and screams – some for my immediate execution. The bread and circuses of Ancient Rome now wore a façade of justice as they nestled in the folds of the Hampshire hills.

Eventually, a form of silence returned, Hotham then summarised the evidence. He was clipped, ordered, and precise. For each charge he presented, evidence and conclusion. In his words, there was little doubt about my guilt.

The jurors spoke amongst themselves for what seemed to be an entire second, before reaching their verdict. The Judge asked the jury

"If they had reached a verdict upon which they were all agreed."
Mustering my Scottish humour, I sat up with an optimistic air as
though expecting a not guilty verdict. This temporarily flummoxed
the Chairman of the Jury whose mouth opened and closed like
an anxious trout. After a little while he recovered his composure,
sending me an icy stare.

The assembled throng were a deep, dense, silent hush.

"We find the accused" said the Chairman of the Jury. The hush
deepened as everyone drew breath.

"GUILTY!"

My eyes scanned the Gentlemen of the Jury, and they were indeed
all landed, monied and male. People of my own class could never
be trusted to sit in judgement on their peers. A slight smile broke
like a gentle wave on my lips. My smile deepened as Judge Hotham
donned his black sentencing hat which tottered precariously at the
apex of the holed horsehair of his wig. He rose from the dais like
a mechanical doll in need of oil, and then began to explain why
I should hang. Among the tens of thousands of words spoken that
day, whether eloquent or other, that small monosyllable clashed
like an almighty clanging gong.

The solemn yet fury flushed justice then proceeded to describe my
crimes which had, apparently "Proceeded from a general malignity
of mind, which has broken out in a desire and a design, not only
to ruin one devoted individual, but to involve every one of this
audience, nay the whole English nation, perhaps, in immediate
ruin. Therefore, you cannot be suffered to live in this world; you

must die. I sentence you to be" there was a noise of hundreds of scarf-wrapped necks turning and craning towards me "taken from this place to the Royal Naval Dockyard in Portsmouth, and there to be hanged by the neck until you are dead. May God have mercy on your immortal soul, and before you go to eternity, for your soul's sake, do what you can, that that eternity may be an eternity of bliss instead of misery."

I gazed upwards as though contemplating my eternal rest, but in truth, it was to allow a hot-fat tear to roll back into my eye. I would not give these good people the sanctimonious pleasure of seeing me break down, repent, and weep. The roof timbers were covered with spiders' webs, beneath which were thousands upon thousands of the smallest holes. I am sure that as I stood, in that moment, death bound, I heard the ticking tapping of the Deathwatch. In my brown coat I was their fellow, a beetle who had almost lain waste to the Hearts of Oak."

In the court Jack may have held back his tears, he did not then.

Chapter Twenty Four

"The shingle still rumbled beneath us, the waves lapped the shore. Jack shook away his ghostly tears, took a long, deep breath and continued.

"Although there were times I struggled with my faith and felt that God had deserted me and many, I did feel that the purpose of us all is to take away sin from the world. My life and travels had taught me the value of human life, and in my own heart I feel that when we truly do love our neighbours we point towards God. My purpose was to bring an end to an ungodly war, and by doing so, to save the lives of tens of thousands on both sides. If I had lived out my life as a painter I would no doubt have gone mad or blind, as the lead and other chemicals did their lethal work; my life, like thousands of others would have been dirty, short, and mean. Well my actual life was indeed brief, but it was thankfully more firework than smoking squib.

With my own eyes I had seen a world which was confused, chaotic, and bloodthirsty. All was black and white, with everything contrary and competing with one another. With my own hands I had attempted to bring order through peace. Although I had failed, and would pay the price, perhaps others would follow, men with sharper wits, more persuasive voices, and minds less fearful than my own.

As they took me from the court, I spoke to those who would listen. I used the words of my friend Thomas. "We have it in our power to begin the world over again." This was my chorus, my refrain as the cart trundled through the thronging thoroughfares. My words were met with hostility by most who jeered and called me traitor or worse, but there were some whose eyes lingered, who heard and perhaps even saw some truth in what I said. I am sure that some, in their turn, went on to preach the doctrine of freedom.

On the day after the trial I was visited by a blacksmith. I knew the gentleman's profession well before he had fully entered my cell, the scent of fire, metal, magic and might preceded him. His square shoulders, shadowed red-rimmed eyes and oak-knotted forearms reminded me of my own father. Strangely, I even called him that twice during our somewhat stilted conversation. He was to construct a cage which would house my dead, tarred body, and needed my measurements to ensure that it was a good fit. Perhaps it was because he practiced the same trade as my father, or since I then had nothing more to lose, I confessed my true name to him, a secret I had kept until that point. He nodded, realising I think, the import of this. "I will mark your name" he said "and place a St. Andrew's cross on the base. God will always be with you." With that he knocked on the door for the guard, and left.

With the mention of the cross, and of my own name, my mind immediately turned to think of my mother. Outside, birds full of spring hope and the promise of new life stirred in the nearby greening trees. It was then a robin began to sing, its' warbled, slender notes skated through the bars. The bittersweet refrain reminded me of my blessed Mother's voice. What had I done to her and my family? Would she and they be damned by association? I *asked the guard for pen and paper, and then with weak hands that could hardly grip I began to scratch a letter to my beloved mother from her prodigal son.*

But where do you begin? It had been five years since I had last seen her. Although I had promised to keep in touch, I had in truth only sent three letters since leaving Edinburgh. None of them contained the truth, the words in those letters were painted more carefully than any sign. Previously, guilt had stopped me nearly every time I tried to lift a pen; I had felt that I was no longer worthy to write to my god-fearing, loving mother. In Winchester gaol, for perhaps for the first time in my life, I set out to write the truth, to tell my story in my own words, knowing that others would - in order to sell their works - distort and sensationalise my actions and cast me as a villain of the ages. Even Mr. Lawrence, although he had promised to tell the truth, would no doubt exaggerate my crimes in order to boost sales. In my letter to Mother the words flowed, at first apology, explanation and then my story. There is so much power in the pen, words danced onto one page and then the next. Fresh candles were brought, and more ink came. The nib scratched, dashed, and dotted.

The letter had covered the trial, described my prison cell and was just about to step into my short future. My hand was raised, the pen was loaded, I hesitated, a ball of black ink formed, rolled, and dripped exploding onto the page.

No! No! No!

In that instant, I knew that I could not, and should not send this to my blessed Mother. Although liberating for me, my epistle would perhaps imprison her because of her association with her rebellious, seditious son. The candle flame flickered and then embraced my tale. A guard watching through the grate hurriedly unlocked and entered, but he was too late. My story, my true story, had become smoke.

Each day the Chaplain, Reverend Westcombe, visited me and the other poor unfortunates destined to be hanged. I sensed it was a chore for him, his conversation was lacklustre, his blessings were insincere, his laboured breathing just about permitting him to finish each, sanctimonious sentence. On each of the three days he called on me he never once looked me in the eye. Did he feel that I was evil incarnate? By gazing into the windows of my soul did he believe that the monster who had wrought havoc on a nation would demonise him, and he too would be damned? Who is to know. What he did wish for, and indeed he refused to grant me communion until he procured it, was a detailed record of all of my works, the more ghoulish, salubrious, and scandalous the better. He wanted to be the one who told my tale, and make a fortune in the process. Pride and avarice. He was just another clergymen, and I had seen many on my travels, who were saints on Sunday, but devils the rest of the week, revelling in all of the seven deadly sins, and carrying out detailed research on others so they may be added to the canon. In my rather tactful manner, I began, to his chagrin, to refer to him as the Perverse Parson, a name which at least made my guard smile. Westcombe never heard my account.

I was besieged by many others, who also wanted my confession, and tales of my adventures. They included the mighty Sir John, who for his own self-aggrandisement, was determined to obtain not only my penance but also my full testimony. I never sought forgiveness from anyone - high or low - for what I did or tried to do. My only regret was that I did not do better. As for my take, as you know I had already committed that to Thomas Lawrence.

Reflecting on my path from tenement to, what some called, treason I concluded that all - please indulge a dead man's generalisation - the misfortunes of men stem from the fact that they do not want to stay in the room where they are told they belong. I had a brief taste of freedom, and became addicted to its flickering flame. Many were of the opinion that a painter should remain behind a brush for every day of his short, poisoned life. But I was damned if I were merely to splash colour on so small a canvas!

But would I be damned? In terms of sins I had committed more than many but far less than some. Needless to say, I will spare the details as even a spirit is entitled to a little privacy. My remaining belongings were sold to pay the gaoler for my bed and board, Ovid went with Mr. Lawrence.

Would my next journey be to heaven or to hell? It was in fact to Portsmouth as in common with many notorious felons I was to be hanged at the scene of (one of) my crimes.

We set off from Winchester at dawn and arrived at Portsmouth Town Gaol just before midday on Monday the 10th of March. A chorus of bells were tolling across the harbour as though proclaiming a holiday and a celebration. It was as though the City had vanquished Lucifer himself. I was released from my manacles which I had worn the past month; my wrists were the dark red of rubbed raw skin and blistered blood. My freedom, however, was temporary, I was immediately bundled into a large, dung-smelling farm cart and tied to a chair. The Chaplain and Gaol Keeper joined me for my short ride.

The crowds thickened and tightened as we approached the harbour where masts rose like a forest of dying trees, pennants, and flags flapping like fish tails. Stalls selling roasted meat and ale were thriving. Many had dressed as though it were a special Sunday; the men in their best frock coats, powdered wigs, and polished boots whilst the women's bonnets and fine dresses caught the breeze. The military and officials on the nearby podium were wearing their medals, badges of office and dress uniforms.

A lump rose in my throat and my eyes began to sting as the long-held-back tears began to flow. My bonds prevented me from wiping my face so I shook my head like a wet dog. Sensing weakness, the faces around me were now more fierce, angrier, larger, their teeth gnashing and crashing like a pack of demons. There were thousands in that place, and undoubtedly many further afield, who wished me dead.

Although my hanging was imminent, there were some who did not appear to want to wait for the niceties, they were more than willing to take the matter of a traitor's death into their own hands. All around me were those with bloodlust in their eyes. Was I to be thrown to them, was I to be torn apart, ripped to shreds? For the first time in my life I knew real fear, pushed by the mob the tumbrel swayed from side to side, pitching heavily, as a boat about to sink amongst the sea of clawing hands.

There was a rush as soldiers intervened lining both sides, bayonets glinting in the grey. There was a shot, so near I could smell and taste the black powder and feel the heat, I closed my eyes and tensed for the inevitable impact; had some soul taken it upon themselves to kill this monster with their own hands? I looked down at my quivering body, expecting, half hoping to see a gaping bloody wound and my life ebbing away.

"Back" barked the troop captain as he held his still smoking pistol high above his head. Almost as one, the crowd seemed to jump, jerkily moving away from the cart. It was then the pelting started. Although it was commonplace for unpleasant items to be thrown at unpopular prisoners, your first dead cat is always a surprise, particularly if it is an ugly brute of a creature with mismatched eyes, a mangy body and sullen expression. Cats gave way to cabbages as rotten vegetables followed. It was as though I was a cooking pot to which the good people of Portsmouth were contributing. I was lucky the Perverse Parson had gifted me an immense nosegay for my buttonhole; the sweet scent did its best to offset the stench.

The crowd were so close that I could feel their collective breath. It was only a thin red line which separated us. I sensed they felt somewhat disappointed that this villain, this most wanted man, this Firestarter had no cloven hoof or forked tail, and the air around him smelt not of sulphur but of slops. Some eyes met mine, a few were looks of pity, most were hatred tinged with a sense of celebration that they had gazed into the eyes of the doomed, demonic Painter. Those around me obviously wished me harm. There was the continued pelting, as well as the catcalls (aye there *are times when the English demonstrate an artful use of language) many of which described in quite vivid detail what they wished to do to my genitals. As they face death some discover faith, when you boil it down what more is there to faith than love? At that moment I had nothing but a form of love for those around me. They had been told that I had meant to hurt them and theirs, but I had not. I had merely sought to end a war. A moment ago, I would have gladly welcomed the warm bloody embrace of death, but the gunshot which I momentarily thought was the last sound I should hear on this earth has roused me. Now I was glad to be alive, I had minutes before I would hang, in plain view of thousands, on the highest gallows ever erected in England, on a mizzen mast taken from the frigate HMS Arethusa. I had limited time, but enough moments, and breath, for now, to sing:*

"Oh, happy band of pilgrims,
Let fear not dim your eyes,
Remember your afflictions,
Shall lead to such a prize."

The lump in my throat had loosened like an Easter tomb. Many say that I was a godless traitor, but would a heretic sing a hymn as the hempen rope was about to be placed around his neck? I had heard tell that freemen of the City of London cannot be hanged with hemp; for them it must be silk. The rope to be used for me was ironically and intentionally one of the few that had survived my fire. Perhaps it sought to exact vengeance for the crimes I had committed against its brothers and sisters. My smiling was another act which offended the throng of what the guards told me were some twenty thousand souls. The crowd wanted me to appear defeated, terrified, and fallen. They wanted, no they demanded, contrition and repentance. Why? So they would forgive? Oh no, it was my humiliation they sought. They hoped that the nearby glint of Death's scythe would cause me to submit. But one should never seek forgiveness for doing what you feel in your heart is right.

My singing offended their ears in more ways than one; this was understandable in its way, I was never gifted with a voice, I was more what you would call keen than capable. Aware of my limitations, I still carried on:

"There is a fountain filled with blood,
Drawn from Immanuel's veins,

And sinners plunged beneath that flood
Lose all their guilty stains:
Lose all their guilty stains,
Lose all their guilty stains;
And sinners plunged beneath that flood
Lose all their guilty stains.

The dying thief rejoiced to see
That fountain in His day;
And there have I, though vile as he,
Washed all my sins away:
Washed all my sins away,
Washed all my sins away;
And there have I, though vile as he,
Washed all my sins away."

I could not remember all of the words, but the final verse was imprinted on my memory. It could well have been written for me.

"When this poor, lisping, stamm'ring tongue
Lies silent in the grave,
Then in a nobler, sweeter song,
I will sing Thy pow'r to save:
I will sing Thy pow'r to save,
I will sing Thy pow'r to save;
Then in a nobler, sweeter song,
I will sing Thy pow'r to save."

The crowd were then momentarily quiet, although they did not look as though they were especially pious, they probably knew what piety sounded like. Sensing that the crowd's fervour had cooled, John White, the keeper of Winchester County gaol stepped forward and, perhaps seeking to rekindle the crowd's enmity proclaimed, "And now for the convicted felon's final words."

In truth, I had not expected to have been able to address the crowd, serious transgressors could not, and I presumed that the authorities would count me in that number. But I, with my newly found voice would not forego such an opportunity.

"When England brought fire, sword, rapine, murder, rapes, and ruin among her colonies, I determined, individually, to burn His Majesty's dockyards, for by crippling the fleet, I would prevent further progress against America. Such was my determination. I acted alone and I almost succeeded. I hate all kings of all nations and denominations. I am proud to say that I am a republican."

The crowd jeered, many of them were red-faced with veins bulging in their red necks. They looked as though they would do themselves a mischief. The hangman had paused allowing me to finish. As best I could, I thanked him for his courtesy.

As the rope was placed around my neck I prayed. For my mother, for my brothers and sisters, and for all of the good people I had met in my two dozen or so years on the earth.

My leaf-thin body dropped. The smoked rope gripped. I clenched my fists, I know not why. On the scaffold it was too late to fight. My thumb, forefinger and then the rest numbed. Round, fat salty tears escaped my eyes finding their way to my dry mouth. The taste dulled, no longer sharp, nothing. Through my closed eyelids colours faded; scarlet, crimson, maroon, purple, charcoal, then black, all black. The sound of the crowd faded, drums muffled, cheers quietened by the breeze, silence wrapped around me. The odour of sea and salt left my nostrils. All other senses were gone but the pain, the intensity of pain remained.

High above the harbour I had danced my final jig, my polished boots kicking fetid air. Until my neck and my body finally broke.

Then silence, calm and an absence of things.

I have no knowledge of how long it was before the silence was broken; the single solemn beat of a drum. Deep, resounding, echoing across the harbour. Gradually the noise began to build, the drum was joined by its fellows, there was music. On a nearby podium a military band played. I looked - oh yes, I could see - around me at the harbour which was still bedecked in celebration. In front of me there loomed a platform; new wood, sawn and shaped, rising above there was a gallows where a red-headed man swung.

The music had stopped. On the podium a round-faced man with stentorian voice began to speak. His medals jangled as he pointed towards the gallows. "Today" he roared "we have seen justice done. The traitorous incendiary has paid for his heinous crimes. The dockyard is working yet." There was a chorus of cheers from all around.

Who was the hanged man? For a while he swayed like washing on a line, but folks soon tire of spectacle. The body was brought down, the rope loosened and a doctor checked for signs of life, he found none. Unchallenged, I had moved silently so I was alongside the doctor. The face which looked into my own was mine.

I was broken. I screamed and howled. I collapsed, I cried until my throat was red-sore, and my tears all spent.

No one looked towards me, no one heeded my cries. A moment passed, the hangman moved towards my corpse, a knife in one hand and a bag blooming with handkerchiefs in the other. The head was lifted and the rope removed. The knife cut deep into one of the arteries of my neck, blood oozed as one handkerchief after another dabbed the flow. Scarlet souvenirs for the ghoulish. This practice was not unique to me, it happened to others equally infamous. Apparently the blood of hanged men was treated as a cure-all. It is the most strange thing to see what happens to one's body after death. I thought of maidens clutching my still warm blood to their breast, I was a young man you remember, and until a short while ago full of life.

Where was I now? What was I now?

Around me the crowd continued to celebrate in the long-established English tradition of drunkenness and gluttony. A well-refreshed soldier walked towards me, ale sloshing from a tankard, in the way of such men he barged straight into me. I expected pain and perhaps a drunken apology - neither. He however grimaced and shivered. Two small boys were zigzagging through the legs of the crowd, they avoided all until they ran into mine. They screamed, pointed towards me then rushed away. I moved through the throng not caring which path I took, all those I carelessly or deliberately walked into reacted in the same way – with a fearful shiver. Had I become an invisible iceman?

As the celebration approached dusk the crowd began to disperse. Many were still rejoicing that the man who was for a winter England's most infamous citizen had been brought to justice. Others, in more cautious voices, spoke of my deeds, and how close, how so very close I had come to success. "What ifs?" were whispered. My very public trial and my yet more open hanging was meant to serve as a warning to plotters, insurgents, and revolutionaries of the dangers of acting in accordance with conscience. But, perhaps for some in the crowd, including those whispering as they drifted home, I had in death become their hope. If one man could do so much to try and right the wrongs of this world, then why not them?

The King and his government hoped to see my death as the final chapter in my story, theirs was to be the final celebration. Oh but, one of the many things we learn from history is that it is usually far too early to celebrate most things."

Chapter Twenty Five

For half an hour, one hour? the effect of the cheap whisky and the few drugs I had been able to swallow had largely worn off. I had sat in silence mostly clear-headed, doing something I had not done for ages. I had listened. Jack sat close by me, his voice now quieter, more reflective.

"For one reason or another I am bound to this place. It do not think it is some sort of divine retribution as I never killed a soul. Perhaps I remain here because this is where my life had its most ripples. I have been forgotten elsewhere, but, for good or ill I am remembered here. Because of that remembrance I remain."

The first words I had spoken in some time were blunt.

"Jack, but you could so easily have been a killer. Your fires may indeed have raged and you could very well have had blood on your hands. It was good fortune, luck." I spat that word. "That saved you, not morality."

"In another time, I could very well have been sent to track you down, after all I have" a pause "no I had, a talent for hunting unassuming men such as yourself. You could very well have been my greatest challenge, but" my tone hardened "it could have been my bullet, and not a rope which did for you."

My words spilled from me.

"After all, is there any real difference between you and those who blew my life apart? You said yourself that you gloried in the sight of the fire you saw from Portsdown Hill. You argue what you did was right, but wouldn't every other bomber, terrorist or revolutionary do the same? I have seen so much destroyed by those just like you! Even if your plan had succeeded what would really have changed? One set of equally bad overlords would have replaced another, just a few years sooner. Oh, and I know about your friend Thomas, the man who was never happy because the real world has no common sense. This world is broken, it was in your day, and it is in mine. I despair."

I stood, then tottered as though to leave. Jack was quickly by my shoulder.

"Although you may think that I and the bombers who blew apart your life and those of many others are the same, we are not. Will, although I had seen so much wanton killing I did not want to take life. I merely sought to destroy those inanimate things which facilitated institutionalised murder. Your enemies seem to have delighted in killing, from what you say, soldier or civilian they do not appear to have drawn a distinction. In my own time, an age where life was cheap and people of my class were lucky to see their thirtieth birthday, I valued life beyond measure. I valued it as the gift it was.

And I do believe in what I tried to do, if I had succeeded the war would have ended many years earlier. Thousands and thousands of lives on both sides would have been saved. I sought to save lives and I fought my one-man war to bring peace.

Although I had bought and carried guns, to me, regardless of what I said earlier, they were theatrical props, to be used to persuade but never to kill or maim.

At some point between one and two o'clock I died a slow and lingering death as though the hangman - or his paymasters - deliberately intended me to suffer, and for me to gaze through pain-clouded eyes at the massed ships in the harbour which represented my failure. Well at the point of death my body ceased to breathe, beat, think, and function. My spirit however still lives, no that cannot be the right word, it lingers here. For what reason I don't know. Do I need to make peace with the cosmos? Or do I just need to make peace with myself?"

So, there we were, in the early hours of All Saints Day, a ghost lingering close to the scene of his very public execution and me, seeking oblivion for the many deaths on my own conscience. I remained quiet, Jack, as though now in a hurry, and sensing the approach of dawn, did not.

"Perhaps not the most obvious, but the very worst thing about being a ghost is that you know <u>everything</u>. Strange as it may seem, we even know the hopes and dreams of those around us. We see the selfish, those who want nothing more than aggrandisement, wealth, power, and control over others. We also see those whose dreams are selfless; they wish to improve the sum total of human happiness. I know you Will."

A few hours before I would have railed against such a preposterous statement, but not then.

"And what I know" his voice now more insistent *"is that eventually we ALL fail. You, I, everyone. But pessimism cannot*

win. The failing of man is that he does not dream enough. Although all dreams do eventually fade to dust, for a brief fragment of time they may be real, they are indications of possibility. We must all learn to dream more, powerfully, possibly. We must dream harder.

Some of us wish to know more than we should. I spent my life seeking answers, but since the hangman took my breath, I have learned many more things, some infernal which I beg each night to forget. But spirits, cursed as they are, cannot. I have met many who roam the earth, some seek others to join them in their solitary, unsettled existence. Bloody-footed Melmouth for instance, who was there when Christ appeared by the tomb, but later denied what she had seen. Damned by an irascible God, she visits those among the living who have reached the depths of misery, and holds out her ice-cold hand. It was She who was in the shadows, summoning you towards her smoke when I first called to you.

It may seem perverse, but as someone who is currently cursed with eternity, even I know that Hades is not a place for residence, it is place of waiting. It is the same for any other place of darkness. Light has a way of breaking through, it may take years, or centuries, but light is unstoppable.

I also know that time is by far the most valuable thing a man may spend, and if I had my short mortal life to live again, I would _live_ every single day of it. Looking back, I wasted too many of my days hoping for tomorrow, but as the singer says tomorrow never comes.

So we must bring light and hope to today. Stories were an anchor for my life. Although we may consign them to children, we older ones also need them to live, to give meaning, significance, and *shape to our existence.*

I never lived a life which was suited to being a father and that is one of my few regrets. Everything is a gift from God, but new life is the highest prize. It should and must be cherished. Although you feel you cannot be the father your daughter Angela deserves that is not for you to judge. She is your reward, and you should treasure her, and love and cherish your wife.

I know this because here in this place I have seen that the blood of each and every suicide covers many faces. What seems like a crime with only one victim is anything but. It has always been the case, death serves as a catalyst for yet more death, as those who have loved the departed themselves seek to escape from the pain of their loss. Even if it is not a physical death, it may well be an end of hope. Eyes cloud with cataracts where love once used to be. Those left see the world through an ever shadowed-sky. Those left feel guilt, their shoulders stooped with the burden of loving words not said, or hurtful ones which were. They regret all but can salvage little and change nothing."

"This place," his arm indicating the harbour, *"is a place where many choose to leave. It is as though the sea lulls them Lorelei like to their doom. Perhaps they feel that the tide will ensure they are soon forgotten. But no, if you have ever been loved others will feel your loss."*

Minutes crept by. I said nothing. Jack also said nothing until the bells announced five o'clock.

"You and I have both served our country. Me, perhaps in a way

that was not clear to it at the time. Some of my life was spent in chains; what did I learn? That in response to rubbing and chaffing the body eventually grows its own protective skin. Although imprisoned I was always free, there were no manacles yet made which could hold my mind. I was fortunate, I saw many others who tormented themselves. I believe that eventually we will all be judged by the eternal jury, our complete truth will then be known. Will, do not judge and sentence yourself. Redemption - in the eyes of others or ourselves - is always possible."

I stood upright. Although everything about me ached, I needed to stretch, to feel as though what remained of me was whole. My mind was in turmoil. I guess Jack sensed that.

"And my friend, always remember that the world is full of contradictions. I cannot recall who told me this tale, but that is by the by. The Truth and the Lie meet one day. The Lie says to the Truth: "It is a lovely day today" The Truth looks up at the azure-blue skies and sighs, for the day was indeed really beautiful. They spend many hours walking together, until they eventually arrive beside a well. The Lie says to the Truth: "The water looks so refreshing, let us bathe together, and wash away our travel dust." Although the Truth is a little suspicious, she tests the water and discovers that it is indeed refreshing but not too cold. They both undress and start bathing. Moments later, quick as lightning, the Lie jumps out of the water, puts on the clothes of the Truth, and runs away. The furious Truth jumps from the well, running everywhere to find the Lie and to recover her clothes. The World, seeing the Truth naked, turns its gaze away, with contempt and rage. The poor

Truth returns in shame to the well where she disappears forever, hiding in the depths. Since then, the Lie has and continues to travel around the world, dressed as the Truth, satisfying the needs of a world which has no wish at all to meet the naked Truth.

Seeking shelter from storms, human or otherwise, I have spent some nights in the damp comfort of caves. One, in the high hills of Derbyshire, I realised when my flint had lit my stubby excuse for a candle was already occupied. An ancient man whose legs appeared to uncoil like rope spoke deeply from the shadows. Sensing danger, I turned back towards the deep black cloud and the slashing rain, as I did so the old-one called "Friend, do not run, what little I have I freely share." We ate, drank, and shared stories, he told me that magic was first born there as he pointed to the creatures and figures outlined on the surrounding walls. He had a voice which your body listened to. He told me of the rocks and the columns which hid in the shadows. "They grow by giving of themselves, drops gather minerals, then fall. In falling the make stalactites and stalagmites, and eventually a mighty pillar. We also grow by falling."

And as for love, your true love, although she has gone for now, when you speak of her you glow, you sparkle, you become who you can be. She has held your heart, and from what I can gather from beneath that façade of yours, she has let you hold hers. Neither of you will ever be the same, you have moulded one another.

Although I was never wed, I knew some fleeting, ephemeral love. There is joy for every one of us in this world, but joy does not knock, the heart's door must always be open to it. Joy is like dandelion wishes, they blow hither and yon. Delight in them my friend, search out and hold onto whatever joy dances on the edge of your eyes before it is gone."

I spoke hesitantly "But I have known many people who have stopped believing in the possibility of joy or hope because of what they themselves had experienced, the loss of loved ones to cruel, cruel diseases, and the weak swept aside as though they were worthless. In the last few years, I have seen so much that is without reason, without compassion, without love. So, although I know Death to be real, hope, God, light or whatever for me is just a phantom, a fairy-tale. How can I live in a world where compassion kills? There have been many times, right now, most of all when all I want for is Death.

But then," I hesitated.

"There are times I wish I could set my thoughts free and stop the clatter in my head. I wish I could be thankful for what I have, not regret what I do not. I wish I could once again sing to my daughter as I did when she was still in her mother's womb, I wish…"

Jack nodded *"You may consider this poor advice, coming as it does from someone who, it could be argued, failed in everything he did, and died before his twenty-fifth year. I believe that you have too much to be another corpse dragged onto the shingle, spending eternity clinging to the thing that has killed you. Whether you believe in the afterlife, or a higher purpose does not matter. Although I discovered one, I am hardly priest material, I do not speak to convert, I merely tell my own story."*

Another pause, longer than the last, did Jack feel that he was losing his battle? Although immortal had he wasted his time on me? He sighed. Ah, and when a ghost sighs it is the deepest most cavernous sound, the echo of the frustration of ages past.

He then spoke slowly, quiet, deliberately. *"When Death's bony finger has reached out towards you but failed to catch hold you live not one but several lives, you are a vessel for the hopes and dreams of the dead. In this liminal space I hear voices of the living, of spirits and those in between. In this harbour which has for so long dealt in death, those voices are powerful. "Live on for me" is the strongest, most repeated refrain. The fallen call to their comrades from wherever they fell, they call from beneath the clay, the sand and sea.*

Will, your mind is filled with your own voices. You feel failure, insecurity, guilt, fear, you feel anger towards everything, but most of all you feel anger towards yourself. The voices clamour and call for silence, and an end, but do you think an end will bring silence?"

He looked out across the harbour and sighed once more. He shook his head. I dissolved, curling, contorted and sobbing, eyes flooded, my whole body - flesh and other - trembled. In that moment, I think that I understood myself for the very first time.

"How long have you been away from your wife and daughter?"

"Three months, or so, the days they…" I replied hesitantly.

"So, less than a" he searched for the word *"deployment."*

His eyes fixed me like a nail to a wall.

"But this time you have not been fighting the Taliban, you have been fighting yourself, and my friend" he kept calling me that *"a man does not fight for his life, and the lives of others and then kill himself. Your comrades, living and dead have given you a chance."*

"You may think that my life would be full of regret, a catalogue of "what ifs?" and "what might have beens?" would my life have been more fulfilled if I had stayed in the Colonies and worked with Thomas to spread hope and resistance? Should I have stayed close to family in Edinburgh? Should I have really tried to become a legendary highwayman? What if I had succeeded in destroying the rope-houses and dockyards of the Royal Navy? So many questions." The smile which he had lost for a while had returned. *"Who knows is the answer. But what I do regret is that I danced alone, my shadow had no twin, there was no echo, no response to my call. I wish that I had found love. You have found what I did not, do not give up on life's greatest gift."*

"One final thing," his voice had softened over the hours, as we swapped tales between the dusk of Halloween and the dawn of All Saints Day.

"I have seen people who just wanted to live, to be free, to build a future. I saw their hope trampled down by mercenaries, by old men who did not listen, blinded by their own bigotry and foolishness. I fought to bring this to an end, my life became a daring adventure and my credo "If there must be trouble, let it be in my day, that the children may have peace."

"We should not be mere clocks that tick and tock our lives away. We must honour those who have gone before. We must not live in

slumber. We must wake one-another, we must ring like bells."

He once again looked out across the harbour, the sharp clear night with its bright moon was melting in the east into the gold of early morning, and a fine drizzle. Jack's eyes widened, he pointed. Suspended over the shadow of the Isle of Wight was a rainbow in the dark, a moonbow.

"My friend, they are the rarest of things, a promise held high in the heavens. The rainbow may not come when you think it should, but it will, indeed, it has come. Hold it in your heart. Now, go home my friend."

With that the brown coated man, my friend Jack faded into the glow of the dawn.

Chapter Twenty Six

An ex-girlfriend of mine became a trapeze artist, now I know this may seem like a somewhat incidental fact but, we all balance on our own high wire. For some the distance to safety is small, reachable. For the rest of us, the rope snakes off into the mist, the wind buffets, and the cable buckles with time and tread. We may fall into the great beyond at any moment. The reality we inhabit is random, but in that existence there are opportunities. Jack gave me a chance.

Immediately after my encounter with Jack I struggled. Was he real or just a figment of my always fertile imagination, perhaps a song lyric which had taken shape? The doubts, the failures, and the desire to leave this life kept returning to me like a high tide. So, a few days later I found myself by a railway line, a stretch that was long, flat, and swift with scrubby buddleias and overhanging trees alongside providing cover. It was mid-morning and the single light of an approaching train was speeding towards me. My heart was pumping, all I needed to do to end the pain was take five steps to the right. I counted down, five, four, three. Two never came, there was a jolt as I was pulled in towards the steel of the security fence. The blue and orange of the train flew by. In the slipstream a powerful, puffa-jacketed woman with an incredulous dog asked me what on earth I was doing. I was then too numb to answer, but tea and cake - which she kindly bought for me in a café by the football ground - helped my words and tears to come.

The next Sunday, a week or so after Jack and I met, I drifted towards a Remembrance Day Service. They are a very British mix of marching children: scouts, cadets, and brigades together with their proud parents; and sharply-creased and highly-polished veterans marching as best they can with their gleaming medals and old memories. Completing the procession are the shuffling civilians. I was a veteran, wrinkled and unpolished and although I felt as though I did not belong, some force compelled me to join the fringes of the parade. There was no dress uniform or smart dark suit for me, just my wrecked combats, my boots held together with cardboard and gaffer tape, and my stale bread face crusted with weather, worry and war.

The crowd pointed with their eyes, accusing me of discourtesy and dishonour; and those close by retreated as my agricultural scent spread. Discontent murmured until their gaze reached my left breast where just above my heart were ribbons and metal, embossed faces glinting in the autumn sun. An older woman, her hair tossed by the chill breeze, looked me in the eye, placed her two hands together as though in prayer and mouthed "Thank you" her lips curled in kindness. Too often we underestimate the immense power of a small act of tenderness - a touch, a kind word, a listening ear, a compliment, or a smile - they all have the potential to turn a life around. My knees buckled as though *I* had been hit by a sniper's bullet, I crumbled and my shambling march stopped. For a moment there were tut-tutted murmurs and whispers before two sets of thick set arms lifted me with the gentleness of doves. "We've got you now son" one whispered in my ear.

I said earlier that Durham was an easy place to leave, it is also the easiest place to return to…and at times when the sun bursts through the leaves and the river ripples words cannot capture its beauty.

Some months ago, I did the bravest thing I have ever done, I asked for help. It took three attempts, two aborted appointments, a hurl of abuse (from me) and a torrent of tears. Post-traumatic stress my counsellor calls it, which is far more common and deadly than you would think. For those of us who have served, we think of the Falklands War as a victory against the odds, what history does not record is that more men who served in the Falklands have committed suicide than died in the war itself. Wounds are many, and the worst are sometimes hidden deep in places the surgeon cannot reach.

One of the two men who have saved me sits and listens, and in his ever-wise way my doctor puts names to absence and gives life to the half-formed things that lurk. He has calmed me and helped me to come to terms with the fact that a person's war is never truly over, it merely changes shape. I am now able to speak. Although my mind is still home to darkness, I now know there are many shades of black. I have exchanged some of my moths for butterflies. I now know that sadness is something which is on me, it will move on, it is not <u>me</u>. Now joy, and not self-harm, is my act of resistance.

And there is always music. I returned to Durham as I had left it, by bus. It was crowded and I pitied the poor unfortunate woman who sat beside me for the six and a half hours. Although cleaner than I had been recently I was far from box-fresh, so I shuffled as far away from her as the window would allow. Her eyes (and nose) appreciated the gesture. All I had to read were two prayer cards, the one my Aunt had given me years before and another which I had picked up in Portsmouth Cathedral a day or so after I met Jack. I gripped the latter, thumb and forefinger rubbing trying to absorb the printed prayer "Enlighten me, guide me, strengthen me, console me." On the back of the card I had written Bear in black ink. When you have little, you mark it all with your own name. "Bear" was Valerie's pet name for me, not only because of my thick coating of body hair, or my love of honey but also because of my occasional sore-headed moods. I hoped that Valerie would forgive her Bear. A heavy tear formed in the corner of my eye.

The woman beside me must have noticed my distress. She offered me a sandwich, apologising in her northern brogue that "They were London ones and didn't have much in them" she was right, but it was tasty enough and I was hungry, the last of my money had been spent on the bus ticket. We chatted, she had been to visit her son at university, he was at Kings College studying psychology (if I remember right) and she was a visibly proud mother. Talk turned eventually to music, I told her that I used to play pubs and the college circuit years before, she too played, her instrument was the flute and she played in some amateur orchestra. The conversation began to dawdle.

"I saw him last night" she pulled a ticket stub from her purse, the name Lyle Lovett meant nothing to me, nodding towards my prayer card she said "and he played this" she, bravely, offered me an earbud which was plugged into an MP3 player.

You will know yourself that music can stop your breath, raise the hair on your neck, cause the body to vibrate with perfect energy, and at times it can be a lightning bolt which strikes the real you, tells of exactly who you are at a precise instant in this headlong rush of life. The fact that someone has felt exactly as you do, and they have had the grace and mercy to share those feelings is overwhelming.

One verse of that song "Bears" connected.

"Some folks drive the bears out of the wilderness,
some to see a bear would pay a fee.
Me I just bear up to my bewildered best.
And some folks even seen the bear in me."

Tears swelled like a tide, irresistible.

"May I listen again?" I must have sounded like a small child.

Twelve repeats later, I thankfully gave the earbud back to the now somewhat disgruntled owner (although she hid it well). A random act of kindness had given this bear the strength he needed.

Jack told me that he stood outside the coffee shop in Philadelphia not daring to go in, well I loitered around the place which used to be my home for nearly a day. I walked around the block so many times I was almost dizzy. Was this a mistake, should I go and this time never come back?

Small feet always seem to drag as though they are much happier where they currently are. Behind me was the sound of happy small feet stumbling in my direction. I moved to one side to let the child pass, she turned, she smiled and the sun came out from wherever it had been hiding the last three or so months. Small eyes widened as her mother asked.

"Are you okay?" The second best of all possible questions. The first followed. "Would you like to come back home with us?"

With Valerie's help I have been able to name the fireworks that are in my head. Some I never wish to lose, but the pain of loss I have turned into the joy of having known Mam, Dad and Phil who now sit in my memory smiling in the many happier times. These are my Katharine wheels, things of beauty. The ugly fireworks still explode, it would be futile to try and stop them, but now they are enclosed, mostly, in a steel box where they can clang and crash to their heart's content but they no longer set the rest of me alight.

And as for my other, what I think are failings, the ever-wise Valerie has an analogy for those. She says they are like car scratches: all cars have them except for those which are brand new or those which only venture out after hours of careful preening and polishing, when there is not an R in the month and the weather is still perfection. Scratches of mind or body tell their stories. Life is nothing without its stories.

My story is that I fought twice, once to protect my country and then to save myself. All wars have alliances, the allies in my own fight have been Jack, then the trainline lady whose name

I can't recall, my beloved Valerie and more recently the kind souls of the NHS. They all have made me better by showing me that I am more than my failures, fears, and regrets, by reminding me that we cannot be wholly liberated from terror and dread, the challenge is to know when to embrace and listen to it, and when to fight it. Black days still come, they probably always will. But the dark will always go, it is not strong enough to resist the light for ever. Although you may cry, scream, howl, and rage, the world is better because you are in it.

I know that for much of my life I have been graceless and less than gracious, I have been and am loved, but have been too arrogant or stupid to realise how thankful I should be for it. An unquiet ghost who was not permitted rest, helped me to realise why I am here, and what may be possible. Every day this new-born yet ragged soul sets out to nurture the good and the kindness in this world. My friend, and I hope that I can call you that, Jack, I hope that you know that you have saved this soul, for that I am forever grateful.

Valerie, Angela, and I, we share our simple joys including a little black dog, a spaniel called Jack, I have now grown accustomed to his barking. We also have our own garden, in it there is a tree which in honour of my arsonist friend we - well Valerie and I - call Liberty, Angela calls it, much more beautifully, "Libertree." At its base are photos, and mementoes of those who when they walked among us were close but are now ash, or are buried beneath the clay. In the shadow of the branches we share memories, tears, music, beer, whisky (not me, I still haven't rediscovered a taste for it), Ribena (Angela's favourite) and laughter. Each spring the once gone return and unfurl in vivid shades of green.

In one corner of the garden there is a wheelbarrow, you never know when you too may need to save someone.

Our family grows. We will blow out the soap bubble of life together, we know that it will eventually burst, but until then we will make it last as long as it can.

Postscript

Now, one of the promises Phil and I made, in the night-soaked conversations we had, was that if one died before the other, the survivor would light one thousand candles to remember all of the others we had served with who never came back. So, in every church I go into I light candles. My favourite place to do this, is for many reasons Portsmouth Cathedral where there is a steel Peace Globe with space for many flames. Whenever I can I place candles there. I am sure Phil, and the others, would approve, even though I have now, wantonly, lit far more than one thousand, and will light many, many more before my time is through.

This story took many years to tell. At first the pen wouldn't, couldn't sit still in my hand. Eventually the words took shape and a year or so later I nervously read the first couple of chapters at a local writers' group. With their help and support the rest of the story fell into place. Just before the book's release I was somehow invited to give a short talk at Portsmouth Harbour, just a few yards from where the book is set, and a short walk from the Cathedral whose battered prayer card never leaves me.

Anyway, at the talk there was a sprinkling of people who listened politely, clapped lukewarmly, paid close attention to the free wine and some of whom even added their names and email addresses to my mailing list.

At the end of the session, as I was packing my belongings into my battered satchel, a man, my age, maybe younger - when you reach middle age it becomes so difficult to tell - walked towards me but stayed ten feet or so away, awkwardly distanced. His eyes swept the floor clean, several times. Not sure whether he wanted to talk to me, "Hello" I said "can I..." He quickly looked up; his eyes were wistful, rheumy, and earnest.

In a rasp of a whisper "Jack saved me too."

My mind stumbled, when it had righted itself, the stranger had gone. Jack's bones might be somewhere in a sack, but his kindness is working yet.

Upon his return to England, Jack could very easily have returned to his trade, and painted out his days keeping his dreams boxed in. But he chose not to. In the unlikely setting of a pub he heard a calling and took it upon himself to play his part in trying to change the world. He chose to live his dreams, he chose to dream by day.

Ultimately, Jack failed, but his actions rippled out. For many he was a villain, for some he became a hero, and for one infamous group of drunken sailors who had liberated his bones from their iron cage, he was a payment for a gambling debt.

In this story are my facts, and the tale of a man named Jack.

Do you know what? I do not think I have properly introduced myself; I am Will Blenkin the narrator of this story. You do not look like the sort of person who would ever enter a Folk Club, but if you do, and you see a fellow with prosthetic arm man wrestling a guitar - and losing - that could be me. If it is, you may hear me sing this, it is based on the Brian Hooper song which I quoted earlier in the text, but I have updated it a little to reflect the truth. It tells the tale of a man history calls a villain, but those who call him that never met him. I had the good grace to meet Jack and I know that he had, and still has, a hero's heart.

You can put bones where you will, but ideas once released
fly free,
The fire in the rope-house was a torch of liberty.
One man died, but many thousands he tried to save
Oh, you may kill a body but freedom rises from the grave.
So, although Jack's bones were in a sack, his torch is working yet.

Such dreams he had, and those rope cannot hold,
to stop a senseless war, the painter fought, valiant and bold.
Touched by freedom's fire, to create the world anew.
To end the course of bondage, the reigns of kings and princes too
So, although Jack's bones were in a sack, his dreams are
working yet.

You can place a body in a cage, tarred and locked up tight,
but Jack's spirt is ever free and walks abroad at night.
Kindly saving souls as midnight bells they chime,
bound to the Harbour to atone for an ancient crime.
But, although Jack's bones were in a sack, his kindness is
working yet.

Acknowledgements & Thanks

There are many contributions which have inspired, informed, and helped to steer the writing of this book. This story was inspired by a chance meeting I had with a book of Hampshire folk songs in The Curtis Museum in the market town of Alton. On the final page of the collection "Folk Songs of Old Hampshire" edited by John Paddy Browne was Brian Hooper's song "The Ballad of Jack the Painter." The song told of a villainous character, a failed footnote in the story of Great Britain, whom the songwriter had lampooned drawing attention to his grisly demise, his inglorious and almost comic after-life, and most specifically his failure. The song celebrated the fact that Portsmouth's "dockyard is working yet." It was probably the triumphalism of the song that struck me, why celebrate someone's death almost two centuries later? Did the song protest too much? Was there more to it?

The song led me to researching Jack's true story; Jessica Warner's "John the Painter" does a brilliant job of pulling together the historical facts. In this story, where the history is correctly stated that is down to Jessica, and all mistakes are my own. Although I read a lot about Jack I still felt that his real motivation for picking up the torch of liberty was somewhat unclear. In my attempt to answer this I looked into the lives of some of the profound thinkers and agitators of the time, primarily the firebrand Thomas Paine. I am indebted to Howard Fast's "Citizen Tom Paine" and Paul Collins' "The trouble with

Tom" who both tell the story of this fascinating, flawed, driven character. Bristol library's newspaper archive was very helpful in providing information on the city's 18th century trade. The staff at Winchester Great Hall provided valuable insight into the building's history and architecture.

The character Will was inspired by some of the folks I met who live on the streets, clinging onto life. Many of these people I met in London where I worked for many years, but it was one particular conversation which convinced me - no, compelled me - to write Will's story. Greg, an ex-army medic was in the centre of Bath; he was kneeling on a sleeping bag, asking passers-by for small change. We talked for a long while about how his life had been broken a few years earlier when he was fighting in a now mostly forgotten war. This once proud, patriotic soldier told me that his life was now measured out in £25 chapters. That amount of money would pay for one night in a hostel where he would have walls, a roof, hot water, warm food, and a brief respite from shadows. Greg told me there were so many more just like him, some of whom I have since met. Books on the wars in Afghanistan and Iraq which have helped to inform my story include Dominic Streatfeild's "A History of the World since 9/11".

There are a number of songs quoted in the book. "December" by The Waterboys has been with me, squirreled away in a corner of my mind ever since I saw the then fresh-faced band play Newcastle back in 1986. Around the same time, my own band Larry and the Actors recorded the Paul & Peter

Simpson song "Thoughts from the backseat of my car", which was released on the compilation album "Twelve go mad in Durham." A recording of the spiritual "There is a balm in Gilead" by the Trimdon Male Voice Choir - of which my much missed dad Jack was a member - was released on cassette tape in the mid-1990s. This tape is one of my most treasured possessions. Although my Dad was not a regular churchgoer whenever he did go he loved to sing old, old hymns, many of these have found their way into the book. Lyle Lovett's version of Steven Fromholz's song "Bears" I first heard during the pandemic, I stopped me then, and still stops me now. The most recent song is one which was specially commissioned for the book, "Painter Jack" by the incredibly talented folk-singer Andy Hill.

Many thanks to family, friends and fellow writers who have helped me to carve these words. Margi Everington who read and encouraged. Karen & Joe Holder and Sue & Martin Dell who provided valuable questions, challenges, and feedback. The good folks at the Whitby Writers' Group. Linda Polkowski who provided the superb cover illustration, Paul Armstrong of the Artistic Lens for the author photo and my very supportive publisher Jon Risdon of Wilfred Books. Last, but by no means least, I would like to thank my darling wife Janet who lived with this story for the ten years or so it has taken me to tell. She has been my rock, a sounding board, my first reader and a constant source of motivation. She has helped to address my many failings in, amongst other things, grammar, and punctuation. I am blessed.

The Songs

As mentioned in the Thanks and Acknowledgements section this book was inspired by Brian Hooper's original song.

The Ballad of Jack the Painter

At the mouth of Portsmouth Harbour, where the old chain
ferry plied,
Some say a spirit hangs in chains where submarines now glide.
Though his bones have gone, the Devil knows where,
Jack the Painter lingers there.
Now Painter Jack's just bones in a sack, but the Dockyard's
working yet.

Though Jack, he was a painter, as a brand he made his name:
He met his fate in Portsmouth, where he set the 'Yard aflame.
But the firemen bold and the seaman brave doused the flames,
the fleet to save:
Now Painter Jack's just bones in a sack, but the Dockyard's
working yet.

At Winchester the trial was held and the sentence it was
passed;
Jack hanged at the gate of the Dockyard from the Arethusa's
mast.
Though the rope store stood a blackened wreck,
There was rope enough for the Painter's neck:

Now Painter Jack's just bones in a sack, but the Dockyard's
working yet.

In chains he hung at Blockhouse Point, and stayed for many
a year,
'til taken to an alehouse as a pledge to pay for beer.
So, if you've no money, just a body in a sack,
You can try for a drink on Painter Jack:
Now Painter Jack's just bones in a sack, but the Dockyard's
working yet.

But, I don't think that it tells the full story, so, I added my own words to Brian's:

You can put bones where you will, but ideas once released fly free,
The fire in the rope-house was a torch of liberty.
One man died, but many thousands he tried to save
Oh, you may kill a body but freedom rises from the grave.
So, although Jack's bones were in a sack, his torch is working yet.

Such dreams he had, and those rope cannot hold,
to stop a senseless war, the painter fought, valiant and bold.
Touched by freedom's fire, to create the world anew.
To end the course of bondage, the reigns of kings and princes too
So, although Jack's bones were in a sack, his dreams are working yet.

You can place a body in a cage, tarred and locked up tight,
but Jack's spirt is ever free and walks abroad at night.
Kindly saving souls as midnight bells they chime,
bound to the Harbour to atone for an ancient crime.
But, although Jack's bones were in a sack, his kindness is working yet.

Although I have written very few songs; my friend Andy Hill has written many. I shared a draft of the book with him, in response, he took Jack's story and told it like this:

Painter Jack

At the mouth of Portsmouth Harbour, where the Gosport Ferry glides.
Some say my ghost still lingers on, along the old dockside.
My name is Johnny Aitken, but call me Painter Jack.
My mortal life is over now, just bones in a tarry sack.

To raze the Royal Dockyards, was my avowed intent.
Seen thousands die in America, across the ocean sent.
Where humble soldiers pay the price, when battle lines are drawn.
But a king without a navy, he can never go to war.

Yes, I fired Portsmouth Rope House, a torch for liberty.
They chased me to North Hampshire, and soon arrested me.
In Winchester they tried me, the sentence was soon passed.
To hang me slow, at the Dockside Gate, from Arethusa's mast.

In chains I'd rot, at the Blockhouse Point, I hung for many years.
Then they took me to an Alehouse, as a curiosity there.

Now I walk the docks at midnight saving lost souls from their fate.
Some kindly words and a guiding hand, I send them on their way.

My name is Johnny Aitken, but call me Painter Jack.
My spirit is forever free, just bones in a tarry sack.
My spirit is forever free, just bones in a tarry sack.

The Author

John Ogden was born in Durham, and raised in the ex-mining village of West Cornforth. In his early twenties he headed south in search of musical fame and fortune which never materialised. He put down his drumsticks and as he was already able to count to four became an accountant. After half a lifetime away he returned to his native North-East in 2022. John now lives with his wife Janet in the beautiful North Yorkshire coastal town of Whitby, where he hopes to add to its considerable stock of stories. Paint it Jack is John's first book.